THE
BUENOS AIRES
MARRIAGE DEAL

BY
MAGGIE COX

MILLS & BOON

All the characters in this book have no existence outside the imagination of the author, and have no relation whatsoever to anyone bearing the same name or names. They are not even distantly inspired by any individual known or unknown to the author, and all the incidents are pure invention.

First published in Great Britain 2009
Harlequin Mills & Boon Limited,
Eton House, 18-24 Paradise Road, Richmond, Surrey TW9 1SR

© Maggie Cox 2009

ISBN: 978 0 263 87442 6

Set in Times Roman 10½ on 13½ pt
01-1009-40812

Harlequin Mills & Boon policy is to use papers that are natural, renewable and recyclable products and made from wood grown in sustainable forests. The logging and manufacturing process conform to the legal environmental regulations of the country of origin.

Printed and bound in Spain
by Litografia Rosés, S.A., Barcelona

hen I leave for Buenos Aires in
days' time you and my son are
ng with me for an extended
holiday…a holiday during which
time a marriage between us will
take place—the marriage that
should have taken place five years
ago!'

'What?'

'You heard me. And when you return to the UK
it will only be for the purposes of winding up
your business and closing it down.'

'Closing it down?'

'Si. It is in trouble anyway, is it not? It can
only be a relief to put it behind you. Once you
are back in Buenos Aires, instead of running
a business you will have to get used to fulfilling the role of my wife instead. Do not worry,
Briana…' Pascual's dark-eyed gleam was deliberately provocative '…there will be plenty
to keep you occupied as far as *that* position is
concerned…'

The day **Maggie Cox** saw the film version of *Wuthering Heights*, with a beautiful Merle Oberon and a very handsome Laurence Olivier, was the day she became hooked on romance. From that day onwards she spent a lot of time dreaming up her own romances, secretly hoping that one day she might become published and get paid for doing what she loved most! Now that her dream is being realised, she wakes up every morning and counts her blessings. She is married to a gorgeous man and is the mother of two wonderful sons. Her two other great passions in life—besides her family and reading/writing—are music and films.

Recent titles by this author:

BOUGHT: FOR HIS CONVENIENCE OR PLEASURE?
PREGNANT WITH THE DE ROSSI HEIR
THE SPANISH BILLIONAIRE'S CHRISTMAS BRIDE
THE RICH MAN'S LOVE-CHILD

THE
BUENOS AIRES
MARRIAGE DEAL

To Trish
May your love and appreciation of beauty continue
to lift your spirits and give you wings to fly!

CHAPTER ONE

RETURNING from his morning hack beneath the dazzling Palermo sunshine, Pascual Dominguez cantered into the relative cool and shade of the stables and dismounted. Patting his steed on the rump as a groom promptly materialised, he ordered the young man to turn the pony out into the field after he had seen to him.

He was in good spirits. After a family party last night in honour of his forthcoming marriage he was looking forward to having his fiancée Briana to himself again in a couple of hours, after she had finished work.

There had been far too many people there last evening for them to grab even one moment together, but tonight they would be having dinner at his favourite restaurant, and afterwards he fully intended that she would be spending the night with him, prior to enjoying a few days together before the wedding.

Time alone away from no doubt well-meaning family and friends…just the two of them.

Briana had turned Pascual's well-ordered world upside down and that was a fact! Never having dreamed that such a powerful instant connection with a woman would ever come his way, every day he woke and counted his blessings.

From practically the moment he had set eyes on the young English nanny his friends Marisa and Diego de la Cruz had hired to take care of their baby girl, Briana Douglas had become the sole focus of all his hopes and dreams. She had consented to become his wife, and now he found himself counting the days to their wedding.

Whistling softly beneath his breath, he found his housekeeper waiting for him as he strode through the opened double doors of the main house. A frown puckered the friendly, still smooth olive-skinned features that belied her years.

'What is it, Sofia?' Pascual arched a dark brow, an inexplicable dart of apprehension shooting through him and making him feel suddenly cold.

'Señorita Douglas came by while you were out riding…' the older woman began.

'Where is she?' he interrupted, gazing impatiently round the stunning marble vestibule.

'She did not stay, señor.'

The housekeeper was delving inside the pocket of

her long black skirt for something. In the next instant she handed Pascual a slim white envelope. *The cold feeling inside him deepened to ice.*

'She told me to give you this letter.'

'*Gracias.*' He all but snatched it from her hand and headed towards the grand winding staircase, taking the steps two at a time before she'd barely finished speaking.

In his personal suite of rooms, he started to rip open the envelope, now frankly *hating* the presentiment of doom that seemed to be clutching his vitals in a vice. *What was wrong with him?* Was he coming down with something? With his wedding only days away, he sincerely hoped not. Standing by the opened balcony doors of his sitting room, he felt a gentle welcome breeze that carried the enticing scents of jasmine and honeysuckle ripple across the single page of cream vellum notepaper that his hand clutched so avidly.

As he started to read, the icy sensation that had gripped him sickeningly intensified.

Dear Pascual

Where do I start? This is so hard for me to tell you, but I have decided that I can't go through with our marriage after all. It's not because I have fallen out of love with you or anything like that. My feelings are still as strong as ever.

But I have increasingly begun to realise that a marriage between us could never really work. The reason is that our backgrounds and who we are as people are just too different. I've tried discussing this with you, but you always tell me there is nothing to worry about and I am just inventing problems where there are none.

I'm afraid you're wrong. Ultimately our vast differences can only impinge negatively on our relationship. Already there have been repercussions within your family because you want to marry an outsider. They mean the world to you, I can see that, and I don't want to come between you and for you to gradually grow to resent me because of it. So, rather than cause any worse heartache by staying and watching what we have slowly disintegrate, I have made the decision to go back to England and resume my life there.

I realise this news will come as a tremendous shock to you, and I am so sorry for any hurt or grief I may cause, but I believe that ultimately this is the right decision for both of us. You have been so good to me and I will never forget you, Pascual, no matter what you might think as you read this letter. I'm also sorry that you have to be the one to tell everyone that the wedding will not be taking place after all—

but, having come to know your family a little, I am certain that this news will only confirm their beliefs that I was totally unsuitable for you in the first place.

Please don't try to contact me again. That's all I ask. It would only prolong the pain for both of us, and I think it's best if we just make a completely new start. Take care of yourself, and I wish you only good things—now and always. All my love
Briana.

'Dios mio!'

As wave after merciless wave of disbelief, hurt and disappointment submerged him, Pascual scanned the letter again, hardly able to take on board the devastating contents that had been so cruelly revealed to him. *She had left him...* Briana— the woman of his heart—the beautiful girl he had fallen so hard for almost on sight and had been going to marry—had left and gone back to England, without even having the guts to tell him to his face the unbelievable decision she had made.

Last night at the party she had seemed so happy. *Hadn't she?* Now he remembered that later on during the evening at his parents' house she had been looking a little tired and strained, and he had longed to get her alone and find out what was troubling her.

In the end—because his friends had not wanted him to desert the party too early—he had conceded to stay and had got his chauffeur to drive Briana home, thinking he would see her tonight and get to the bottom of her disquiet then.

It was too cruel to realise that his intention would now never materialise because she had elected to leave rather than wait and talk to him. *Why had he not listened to what she had tried to tell him before?* he asked himself, anguished. Clearly Briana had believed there definitely *were* problems, even if he had not. But how dared she assume that she knew what was 'ultimately best' for both of them? She was merely speaking for herself...not for him!

Suddenly feeling that the generously sized room had become a stifling prison, the growing need inside him to escape and breathe some fresher air galvanised him into unhappy action. Throwing the letter down on a nearby bureau, he once again went outside. A violent expletive left his lips as he strode purposefully out into the hot mid-morning sun, the heels of his hand-crafted, made-to-measure calf leather riding boots ringing out clearly on the bleached white cobblestones before him.

For the second time in his thirty-six years he had been brought starkly face to face with what loss meant and it had left him reeling. The year he had turned thirty his best friend Fidel had lost his life in a horrific car crash, leaving behind a wife and child.

Pascual had been brutally awakened to the fact that life was short—and what was the use of having great wealth at his fingertips if he had nobody significant to share it with? Soberly he had reflected on the future and realised that he craved a wife and family of his own. But in his hopeful search for a mate it had unfortunately transpired that he had given his heart to a woman who had clearly thought so little of his feelings that she imagined it was nothing to him for her to simply walk out without warning or giving him proper explanation.

Again it hit Pascual that Briana had left and such was his agony of spirit that for a moment despair almost brought him to his knees. Why had she not trusted him enough to talk to him about her doubts for their future—if doubts were what she had had? As far as he was concerned right now, her actions put her beneath his contempt! His only consolation was that he hoped she would come to bitterly regret her hasty desertion of him and suffer accordingly.

Because he would not go after her… Not for a second time would he invite her rejection of him—no matter how desperate he might become to see her again in the following few days, weeks, years. *And if he ever happened to discover that she had left him because of the unthinkable…because she had fallen in love with somebody else…then he would honestly curse her to the very end of his days…*

Five years later, London, England.

'Was that the postman, love?'

'Yes, Mum.'

Staring down at the slim brown envelope that she'd retrieved from the mat, Briana felt her heart drop like a lead weight inside her chest. If she wasn't mistaken it was another missive from the bank, and this time maybe the threat of a court summons that had been hanging over her head for weeks now had become a horrible reality.

Just eighteen months ago the hospitality business she had set up, providing administrative and organisational services for visiting business people from abroad, had been flourishing almost beyond her wildest dreams. But since the threatening global recession had taken a grip the way Briana's thriving business had started to plummet was no joke. People were not so eager to use less well-established businesses like hers when other, more long-standing companies could risk undercutting their fledgling competitors and charge less for the same services.

She had a son to raise and rent to pay—and how was she going to do either of those things when there was barely enough money coming in to feed them, let alone pay bills?

'Briana? Are you going to come in and have some

breakfast with me and Adán before you leave for your weekend away?'

'Of course. Just give me a minute, will you?'

Stuffing the offending envelope unopened into her bag, Briana sighed heavily. She had no intention of sharing with her mother the news that she had received yet another worrying letter regarding her debt. Frances Douglas would sell the clothes from off her back if it would help her daughter and grandson make ends meet, and she had already threatened to take a second mortgage out on her own house to help them. *She had done enough.* Without her help Briana wouldn't have been able to set the business up in the first place. Now it was up to her to get them out of the hole they were in.

Pushing her fingers resignedly through the mane of silky brown hair that seemed to have a mind of its own, she returned to the kitchen with a deliberately cheerful smile on her face. Her young son was seated up at the breakfast bar on a high stool, eating his cereal, and his grandmother was busy slotting two slices of wholemeal bread into the toaster.

The child beamed when he saw Briana. 'Mummy, this is my second bowl!' he happily announced, milk glistening on his small dimpled chin.

'Is it, my angel? No wonder you're getting so big!' Lovingly dropping an affectionate kiss on the top of his silky dark head, Briana started moving away towards the boiling kettle on the marble-effect worktop. 'Cup of tea, Mum?'

'Why don't you sit down with Adán and let me do it? And you're not going out of this house this morning until you eat at least a couple of slices of toast, either! All this worry is making you thin and pale—and how is it going to help anybody if you fall ill?'

'It's not that I'm not eating.' Curling her hair behind her ears, Briana sighed and dropped teabags into the two waiting mugs, 'I've just been a bit distracted, that's all. This weekend simply *has* to go well, Mum. I've got three entrepreneurs entertaining some billionaire from abroad, and I've got to help take care of them in a Tudor mansion I haven't even had a chance to familiarise myself with yet. I have to get there early and get my act together to greet them or I'll be for the high jump! Thank God Tina went there yesterday, to do some groundwork for me! If I impress, it's been hinted that there might be some more work coming my way from that direction—so keep your fingers crossed for me, won't you?'

'You shouldn't need me to keep my fingers crossed!' Frances Douglas announced, her smoothly powdered features gently chastising. 'You are the very best at what you do, Briana Douglas, and don't you forget it! Your trusting nature brought you that bad debt that's got the business into trouble…not your lack of ability!'

'Thanks, Mum. I needed a boost this morning. You're an angel!'

'And don't fret about Adán either. I have a lovely weekend for us both lined up. I just want you to go to work and concentrate on what has to be done without worrying about us.'

'I promise I won't let you down.'

The older woman's light grey eyes glistened. 'You've never let me down in the whole of your twenty-seven years, child, so don't even think such a thing!'

Her own eyes moist, Briana sniffed and gave her mother a brief hard hug. *She was so lucky.* She had the most wonderful mother a girl could wish for, and a darling little boy who was the light of her life. All things considered—financial problems aside—she wasn't doing badly. *So why, then, just at the moment when she had determinedly decided to look on the bright side, did a disturbing vision of her child's father slide across the cinema screen of her mind and clamp her heart hard enough and painfully enough to take her breath away?*

The house was startlingly impressive. Set in the napped velvet green of the gently undulating Warwickshire landscape, in what was known as Shakespeare country, it was a genuine beautiful relic from England's tumultuous Tudor past that anyone with half an interest in history would relish.

Pascual had stood outside for several minutes after the chauffeur had opened the door of the Rolls-Royce that had brought him from the airport—simply to admire its black and white three storeyed wattle and daub façade and the small arched windows with their leaded panes. The grounds were stunning too. On the way in they had driven past an imposing gatehouse and parkland, as well as some trees that looked as durable as any fascinating ancient monument he had ever seen. As if to doubly remind him that he was in the English countryside now, and far from the vibrancy, colour and heat of Buenos Aires, rain had started to fall—softly at first, then hard enough to make him immediately dash for cover.

As he did so he literally bumped into a young slim blonde who announced that her name was Tina and that she was working for the businessmen who were hosting Pascual's stay this weekend. After showing him to his suite of rooms she said she would bring him some coffee and refreshments—then her colleague would take him to meet his hosts.

Welcoming the opportunity to shower and take stock of his surroundings before partaking of any refreshments and putting on his 'business head,' Pascual took his time getting ready for his meeting. All the while the steadily falling rain drilled against the diamond-patterned leaded windows of his bedroom and, glancing outside, seeing the boughs of the surrounding trees bend almost to the ground, he realised that the wind was whipping up quite a storm too. But inside it was cosy and warm, and the kind of peace and quiet that he almost *never* experienced at home descended like a soft down blanket, cocooning him from the rest of the world.

His ensuing sigh was almost contented. *After all...what had he to worry about?* However long he made his hosts wait, the last thing they would do would be to voice a complaint. They were getting the chance to buy the most sought-after thoroughbred polo ponies in the business—the elite of the elite—and so they would stem their impatience and relax for however long it took before Pascual finally sought them out.

Absorbed with fastening the small diamond cufflinks on his tailored deep blue Savile Row shirt, he frowned at the sudden knock on the door. No doubt it was the little blonde, returning with his refreshments, he thought lazily. Good. He could do with some strong black coffee.

Outside the panelled oak door in the long, low-ceilinged corridor, Briana was schooling herself to try and breathe more slowly. She'd arrived late, despite all her best efforts, and had just got there in the nick of time to take the tray of coffee from Tina and bring it up to their VIP guest's room. Patting down her hair, she hoped her motorway dash and her lack of time to retouch her make-up would not detract from the warmth and professionalism that was usually her byword. She hadn't even had the presence of mind to ask Tina what their important guest's name was! *Never mind.* Perhaps he'd just be so grateful for the coffee he wouldn't notice that she didn't address him by his name.

The silver coffee pot, patterned cup and saucer and little white jug on the elegant silver tray rattled a little between her hands as Briana held it, and she made herself take another steadying breath.

'Good timing! I was just—*Dios mio!*'

Hooded eyes the intensity and colour of luxurious cocoa set in a handsome strong-boned face with high cheekbones and the most sensuous masculine mouth imaginable stared back at her, as though its owner hardly believed the validity of his own eyesight.

'What in God's name are *you* doing here?'

Just in time Briana held onto the already precariously rattling tray. *Was she dreaming?* As her heart pounded out a shocked tattoo, she had to struggle to maintain her balance. *Pascual was the VIP guest?* How could she not have known that? Suddenly her equilibrium and professionalism fled altogether, and she was left feeling so painfully vulnerable, exposed and inadequate that tears were a mere breath away.

'Did you hear what I said?'

For a moment his accent sounded heavier than

she remembered. The naturally sensuous timbre of that arresting voice still had the power to turn her limbs to the fluidity of water Briana discovered disturbingly. 'I'm working…and I've brought you your coffee,' she managed through numbed lips, giving him a nervous lopsided smile. 'Do you mind if I put the tray down? I'm afraid I might drop it.'

Holding the door wide so that she could enter, Pascual allowed his dark, accusing gaze to follow her like sharpened daggers as she crossed the room to deposit the tray on a small carved oak side-table.

'What is the meaning of this?'

He was studying her as if she were a nasty trick being played on him…a trick he abhorred and detested.

'I told you…I'm here working. Your hosts hired my company to provide hospitality services for your stay. I didn't realise that you were the VIP guest. I'm sorry, Pascual…'

Biting her lip, she felt herself blush hard at the old familiar use of his name and instantly regretted voicing it. Especially when his handsome face demonstrated no pleasure whatsoever in seeing her again…in fact the exact opposite!

'This is probably the last thing you need. Seeing me again, I mean,' she murmured. Her confidence drained away as his eyes tracked slowly and devastatingly up and down her body, in a simple but professional black A-line skirt and jacket, as if checking her out for flaws.

What was he going to do? If he dismissed her and she couldn't carry out her job it would be the last straw as far as her finances and her reputation went. Briana prayed he wouldn't go as far as that. And at the same time as she worried about losing this job—*and laying the hurt of the past aside*—her hungry eyes wanted to weep with joy at the flesh-and-blood evidence of the man she had loved and had secretly dreamed of one day seeing again.

He looked wonderful. 'A sight for sore eyes', as her mum would say. And he'd hardly changed at all—though his stature seemed more imposing than ever. His physique was still leanly muscular, and underneath the sublimely tailored clothes he wore no doubt still in tip-top, enviable condition. And with that arrestingly gorgeous face Pascual Dominguez was not the kind of man who appeared on a girl's radar every day. At least not where Briana came from.

Right from the start she had been smitten, and in no time at all had found herself blissfully and madly in love with him. When she'd discovered that he felt the same way about her she had hardly been able to believe her luck. *But that had been five years ago—five years in which she'd had to come to terms with being a single mother, because Pascual had no clue that he had fathered a child with her when she left.* Not a day went by when the dreadful guilt of that reality didn't weigh her down…

When he still didn't speak, but continued to stare at her as if not knowing whether to shake her senseless or verbally rip into her until her ears rang, Briana twisted the suddenly chilled fingers of her slim hands together and glanced back at the ornate little table where she had put down the tray she had brought. 'Shall I pour you some coffee?'

'Forget the damn coffee! What do you think you're playing at?'

His bitter, chastising tone shocked her blood to ice. 'I'm not playing at anything. This situation is as unexpected and shocking for me as it is for you.'

'But you *did* play me for a fool—didn't you Briana?' His dark eyes narrowed furiously beneath their long-lashed hooded lids. 'I still find it hard to believe you did what you did…even after all this time!'

'It was never my intention to make you feel like a fool.'

Feeling her lips tremble, Briana desperately sought to hold it together—not to break down in front of him and confess all. What would it serve to fully explain now why she had left him? Five years had passed by. He hadn't wanted to listen to her then, so why should he listen now? Anyway…right then she was hardly prepared or willing to rake over old coals and engage in a row—which was no doubt what would happen. As for Adán's existence—she *couldn't* tell him about that just yet. She needed more time…

'I'm really sorry things turned out the way they did, but perhaps it was for the best?'

It was a *stupid* thing to say, and it sounded totally banal.

'For the *best*?'

The words reverberated round the room on a savage breath, and Briana registered the emotion Pascual was feeling like a punch. Confusion, anger, frustration…it was all there.

Scraping his fingers agitatedly through silken layers of rich dark hair, he moved his head from side to side, staring at her hard. 'I can get over being made a fool of in front of my friends and family, but what I *cannot* come to terms with or forgive is that you gave me no indication that your professed feelings for me could be broken off so easily. Or that you would leave without even giving me a chance to hear why from your own lips instead of reading it in some cold, unemotional letter! You must be a consummate actress, Briana… You seemed happy and in love and I believed you. What an idiot I was!'

CHAPTER TWO

His heart was thundering as hard and as fast as any express train. It was difficult to take in the fact that the woman he had once loved, who had so callously deserted him mere days before their wedding, was standing there in front of him.

Pascual discovered that his memory of her had not served him as well as he'd thought. In the flesh Briana Douglas was far more beautiful than any mental picture he could call up. Right then she reminded him of an exotic intense port wine, and even though he deplored what she had done he still wanted to drink in every inch of her until he was intoxicated. She had always had a figure to make his pulse race, and in the slim pencil skirt and smart tailored jacket she wore he saw that it was Marilyn Monroe hourglass perfect. Her very presence exuded an earthy sexiness that heated his blood. Would heat *any* man's blood! *But it was her face that arrested his attention the most.*

With her almost feline smoky-grey eyes, apple cheeks and lush enticing mouth, she was a woman to entertain the most sensual private fantasies about. With that face and body she would stop rush-hour traffic in any major city of the world in a heartbeat. Suddenly Pascual was intensely excruciatingly jealous at the idea of her with somebody else—the idea that she might have left him because she preferred another man to him. It took him a moment to get his bearings as well as his sudden inconvenient and shocking desire under strict control.

'There must have been some other reason you left me besides the one that you stated in your letter. Did you leave me for another man? Is that it?' However controlled he strove to be, he still had to voice the question that had been burning in his mind all these years. She flinched, and his gaze clung to hers, fear of her answer making him as tense as a string on a harp.

'Of course I didn't! I'm sorry if you thought that, but there was no one else…there still is no one else.'

Exhaling a long, relieved breath, he was still infuriated by her apparent calmness when inside everything in him was churning as turbulently as the Atlantic in a squall.

'And what about you?' she ventured tentatively. 'Did you get back with your ex?'

'My ex?'

For disturbing seconds Pascual re alled something that had happened the night before Briana had left. The Brazilian model he had briefly dated before he had met her had unexpectedly turned up at the family party, on the arm of his cousin Rafa. His mother, being the perfect hostess, had not turned her away. During the evening Claudia had drunk a little too much cachaca, and when Briana had been out on the terrace talking to Marisa and Diego she had pulled a stupid stunt on him. She'd circled his neck with her arms, pressed her body hard against his and kissed him full on the mouth…

Pascual's blood ran briefly cold as he remembered the incident with renewed distaste and anger. He wasn't remotely interested in taking up with Claudia again…either then or now. It was Briana he had loved. But clearly she had not loved *him*. Why else had it been so easy for her to walk away? The idea pierced his very soul. No man liked to think the loving relationship he believed to be real was based on a lie. A lie that meant his sweetheart did not feel as strongly for him, her lover, as she had insisted she had. Renewed hurt and fury coursed through his bloodstream that the woman in front of him had treated him so abominably.

Raising her bewitching gaze to his, she attempted a smile of sorts. She wasn't quite successful, and he saw the worry and concern reflected clearly in her eyes. *Good.* He was glad he had unsettled her. God knows, she had unsettled him!

'When she showed up at that party…I just thought that you and she—'

'Well, you were wrong. She was dating my cousin and he brought her with him. End of story!'

'Well, then…I'd better just leave you to have your coffee,' she remarked. 'Your hosts are waiting for you in the drawing room downstairs. Shall I tell them you'll be ready in about twenty minutes or so? I can meet you in the lobby and take you to them.'

'I will be ready when I am ready, and not before!' Pascual snapped, turning his back on her and moving towards the tray of coffee.

Choosing to remain silent for a few moments, he poured some of the hot aromatic beverage into the porcelain cup and took a sip. Definitely particular about the type of coffee he drank, he found he could not fault whoever had chosen this particular blend on his behalf.

Facing Briana again, he observed the slight pink flush across her cheekbones. 'You are here the entire weekend?' he asked, knowing this conversation they had started had only just begun.

'Yes…my job dictates it.'

'And how long have you been working for this company that provides "hospitality services"?'

'About three years. It's my own company.'

'So you are a businesswoman now? You have managed to surprise me again!'

Unable to keep the cynicism from his voice, Pascual was actually genuinely taken aback by the revelation. The Briana he had known had never given any indication of being remotely interested in starting up her own business. Back then she had vowed she was only happy working with children and animals. On her arrival in Buenos Aires she had found work as a professional dog-walker, then as a children's nanny. But he had learned to his cost that she had not been entirely frank with him about many things, and her dishonesty still cut him to the quick.

'I'll leave you to enjoy your coffee in peace and go and wait downstairs.'

Moving towards the door, Briana could not disguise her eagerness to get away, and it incensed Pascual that she should want to effect distance between them again.

'Before you run away I want you to tell me something of these businessmen I am meeting with No doubt you have some information that might be useful?' Staring at her pointedly, he knew a sudden desire to test her out and see if she was at all competent at the business she had chosen for herself. If he himself had been in this line of work the first thing he would want to know was about the kind of people who were employing his services.

'What do you want to know?' she asked, clearly discomfited that she could not escape as easily as that.

'I want to know the things they have *not* revealed in their bid to buy my horses. You know the kind of information I am getting at? It is important that my ponies go to the very best homes. As I am sure you are aware, I do not make these transactions just for money.'

'All their credentials are first class, but if you want to ask me about specifics fire away. I can assure you that I've done my homework in that regard.'

'Really? But you clearly did not know that it was *me* that was the VIP guest this weekend, did you? Is that not somewhat remiss of you?'

A scarlet brand seared even hotter colour into her cheeks. 'It wasn't a mistake I would ever make normally, I can assure you! It's just that I've had a lot on my mind lately, and I—'

'Your personal concerns should never impinge on your ability to do your job well.'

'In a perfect world that might be so, but in case you hadn't noticed this world *isn't* perfect, and from time to time people *do* have worries that cannot help but disturb them.'

'What kind of worries do you have nowadays, Briana?' Pascual shot back, no small amount of bitterness edging his tone. 'I thought you must be perfectly happy and content. After all…you escaped from a man and a marriage you clearly did not want, did you not? I imagined that you must have got *exactly* what you wanted when you walked out on me.'

'Can we *not* do this? It's painful enough that we should meet up again like this without us sniping at each other. We're both here for more important reasons than what's between us personally. I know we need to talk, but this is hardly the right time.'

Wanting to, but hardly able to refute her argument right then, Pascual took another sip of his coffee, then placed the cup and saucer back on the tray. 'Give me five minutes and then I will meet you downstairs,' he responded tersely. 'No doubt we will indeed have an opportunity to discuss our personal issues over the weekend. If it looks like we will not—then we will have to make sure we create an opportunity. I can assure you of one thing: you are not leaving this establishment until I hear the full account of why you ran away from our marriage. And even then I will not let you go until I am satisfied that you have told me the truth!'

After her encounter with Pascual, Briana was still inwardly shaking as she attempted to chat to Tina in the lobby, and she knew her colleague saw that she was unusually distracted. Priding herself on her ability to remain unflappable in most situations— especially when it came to her work—she feared she was going to have to dig deep for resources she wasn't even sure she had to get her through the rest of *this* weekend.

When Pascual descended the thickly carpeted staircase, only moments later, her breath all but got locked inside her throat. If he'd meant to make a statement that there was no question it was *he* who was the VIP guest this weekend, then he had more than succeeded. He had teamed the most exquisite bespoke black jacket with beautifully tailored trousers and a deep blue shirt, and Briana's knees almost gave way beneath her at the sight of him. He had always looked amazing in a suit—elegant in a way that most very masculine men couldn't attempt to carry off, as well as effortlessly stylish, fit, and sexy enough to make a woman forget what she was thinking about the second she clapped eyes on him. No matter what her age or marital status!

It was no surprise when Tina leaned over to her and whispered, 'My God! He's the most *gorgeous* man I've ever seen. How lucky are we that he's the VIP client!'

Lucky? That wasn't exactly how Briana would describe what she was feeling as Pascual turned his disdainful dark gaze her way and silently warned her that he was not finished with her yet…not by a long chalk.

'Señor—Mr Dominguez…your meeting is this way. Please come with me.'

As she led him into the elegant drawing room where the three businessmen were waiting to meet him, they rose in unison from their pin-tucked armchairs round the fireplace. Her voice had a slight tremor in it as she made the formal introductions. There was no doubt in her mind that the men were relieved that Pascual had finally appeared, and straight away she sensed how deferential they were towards him. Her ex-fiancé had always seemed to elicit that kind of response from other people. There was something almost *aristocratic* about him that, along with his sensational looks, guaranteed he commanded instant attention wherever he went.

After five years of not seeing him the impact he made when he walked into a room had not lessened one iota, Briana discovered, and she wondered what Tina would say if she ever found out that this 'gorgeous man', a wealthy Argentinian, was the father of her little boy Adán. Surveying him now, she could hardly believe it herself. Their whirlwind romance seemed such a long time ago. A long, *lonely* time ago, she thought with a sudden profound ache in her heart.

'Can we get some more coffee in here—and maybe some brandy, sweetheart?' Steve Nichols, MD of an advertising agency in Soho and lately co-owner with his two colleagues of highly desirable stables in Windsor, took Briana aside.

Glancing into his pale blue eyes and looking at his slightly shiny pallor, she couldn't help shivering with distaste. Unfortunately she knew his type. He might be on a business trip, but he would consider any reasonably attractive female between the ages of sixteen and forty fair game. Briana knew she would have to keep her wits about her around him. His business credentials might be impeccable, but that didn't mean his manners or his behaviour towards women followed suit.

To Pascual—a fellow entrepreneur, with a commodity to sell that he very much desired—he would be sycophantic and deferential to a tee. But to her and Tina he could potentially be a nuisance.

'Of course… Was there anything else?' Glancing deliberately over at the other men she waited until they all agreed that coffee and brandy was just perfect for now.

As she turned to leave Steve Nichols leaned over to her and whispered conspiratorially, 'Hurry back, sweetheart,' and winked. At that very moment she sensed Pascual's deeply disapproving gaze come to rest on her, and then on the man beside her. Briana's face flamed again. She hoped to God he didn't think she was *encouraging* him!

The meeting went on for at least three hours, and by then it was nearly dinnertime. The hosts had requested that dinner be provided and catered for by a local well-known Michelin-starred restaurant, and while Briana and Tina dealt with the staff from there, who had arrived with their supplies and were currently ensconced in the house's ample kitchen, the three businessmen retired to their respective rooms to get ready.

To be honest, Briana was glad of the breathing space in which to busy herself with the practicalities of her job and stem the tide of anxiety and emotion that had swept over her since she'd seen Pascual again. *But she knew she couldn't avoid him for ever.* Sooner or later he would confront her about the events of the past and the unexpected and abrupt manner in which she had left Argentina.

He would demand a fuller account of *why* she had left.

The plain fact of the matter was that her reasons for leaving had not become any easier to come to terms with over the years. In fact, some days she worried that they would be with her, spoiling her chance of happiness with a man, for ever… Not that she even *wanted* any other man. After all that had happened, Pascual's trust in her was obviously going to be in very short supply. Would he even believe her when she *did* finally explain things?

About halfway through the evening Tina emerged from the private dining room that overlooked the beautiful gardens which now, as darkness fell, were hidden from view by the heavy velvet drapes at the windows. Briana rose up from the padded love-seat in the lobby and asked, 'How's it going in there? Everybody happy?'

'The food looks amazing! Everyone is tucking in, but our gorgeous Argentinian looks bored, frankly— as if he'd much rather be somewhere else than here.'

Briana's stomach sank. Their personal business was one thing, but if Pascual was looking bored then the businessmen who had hired her company's services would not be so thrilled, and she felt responsible for that. Somehow she had to rescue the situation.

'I was thinking everyone might like to go out somewhere afterwards. There's a private members' club with a casino in town. I've already been on the phone to them and they would be more than happy to have our party visit.'

'Great idea! Why don't you go in and tell them?' Tina replied, with a wink of her plum-coloured eyelid. 'They'll probably appreciate the suggestion more coming from you... I've noticed how they've all hardly been able to take their eyes off of you— *especially* the heavenly Mr Dominguez!'

'You're imagining things.'

'All I know is if I had even *half* the sex appeal you've got, Briana Douglas, then I'd be milking it for all I was worth! Every one of those men in that dining room is a multimillionaire, and Mr Dominguez— who's by far the yummiest of the lot—is apparently a *billionaire*! Haven't you ever fantasised about some

outrageously rich and gorgeous man sweeping you
off your feet and marrying you?'

Briana would have laughed out loud if the irony
of her colleague's words hadn't been quite so acutely
painful. Touching her fingers briefly to her burning
cheek, she dismissed the younger girl's comments
with a deliberately distracted air, and gave the black
velvet waistcoat she wore over a white silk blouse a
little tug to bring it better into alignment with the
waistband of her matching fitted skirt.

'I'll go in and talk to them... In the meantime,
Tina, could you get me a cup of coffee and a
sandwich from the kitchen? I don't think I could face
a meal tonight. Do you mind?'

'You're mad, turning down the chance to try some
of that fantastic food that's been brought in! They
brought enough for us with them, you know.'

'Then why don't *you* have my share?'

Heading down the rich maroon carpet of the
hallway that led to the dining room, Briana thought
she'd be hard pressed even to eat the sandwich she'd
requested, let alone a full meal. Her stomach was
deluged with butterflies at just the thought of having
a private conversation with Pascual, as she knew she
must. She felt doubly unsettled when she thought
about her little son...the child he had no idea that
he'd fathered when she'd left Argentina in such an
unseemly hurry. Following on from that came the re-

alisation that someone with the wealth and status *he* had at his fingertips could all too easily take Adán from her if he had a mind and a will to…

'A casino? What an inspired idea—if you don't mind my saying so, Miss Douglas!' Steve Nichols leant back in the rather grand Tudor dining chair he occupied as his colleagues readily concurred, and gave Briana another one of his irritating winks.

Compressing her lips in mild irritation, she quickly glanced round the rest of the table and endeavoured to engage the other diners with her pleased smile. But the gesture faded prematurely when her anxious gaze inevitably collided with Pascual's. He did not simply look bored, as Tina had suggested. Quite clearly he was more annoyed than anything else! Was that because she had walked in and soured his mood?

Once upon a time his face had lit up whenever she came into a room where he happened to be, and again Briana's heart couldn't help but yearn for those happier times. To be young and in love with the man of her dreams, living in a vibrant and amazing city like Buenos Aires, had been *more* than incredible! Sometimes she had to pinch herself to remember that it had ever happened at all… Perhaps it was something she'd dreamt up, because of her loneliness now? But she only had to glance at her son's sweet dark-eyed face to see the startling resemblance to his charismatic father, and she told herself to simply count her blessings. Having Adán reminded her that she hadn't lost everything, after all. She had her precious child.

'What about you Mr Dominguez?' she forced herself to ask. 'Would you like to go the casino?'

'Only if you will agree to accompany me, Miss Douglas,' he answered smoothly, with an arch of his eyebrow. 'I always like to have a beautiful girl on my arm when I go to a casino…for *luck*, you understand…'

'I…I'm afraid I have work to do.'

All eyes were upon her, and Briana wanted the floor to open up and swallow her. *What was Pascual playing at, inviting her to go with them?* He must know it was completely inappropriate and would put her in a most awkward position.

'Come, come, Miss Douglas,' coaxed Mike Daniels, one of the other businessmen. 'Mr Dominguez is our guest tonight. He's come all the way from Argentina for our meeting—the least we can do is grant him this one request, don't you think? Think of it as one of the perks of the job. Myself and my colleagues will gladly foot the bill.'

Still doubtful, Briana easily guessed that Pascual was taking the utmost pleasure in her obvious discomfort and embarrassment. She wanted to tell Mike Daniels that acting as escort to his VIP guest on a visit to a casino was definitely *not* part of the services her company provided. But she sensed her ex-fiancé's potential to make life very difficult all round for everyone if she refused.

Her grey eyes beseeching, she gazed back into the compellingly handsome face that still lazily studied her, and disturbingly saw that a small mocking smile was playing around his lips.

'I haven't brought anything suitable with me to wear to a casino.'

'What you have on is absolutely fine.' Her tormentor's smile widened, and his dark eyes lit with mischief as he deliberately swept his gaze up and down her figure, letting it linger in particular on the lush curve of her breasts outlined by the snug black velvet waistcoat.

His aim was obviously to embarrass and belittle her as much as he could, Briana saw, and she would have had no bones about demonstrating her fury with his behaviour if only they had been alone. As things stood, she couldn't do that. Not without making a scene and besmirching her hard-won reputation as a professional businesswoman.

'Very well, then. I'll go and ring the casino and let them know how many of us are coming.'

CHAPTER THREE

THE private members club was situated in an elegant Georgian house tucked away down a quiet country lane, and it welcomed them with open arms. Used to his name and his wealth opening doors Pascual hovered conveniently close to Briana's slim back as they were shown into the private casino that was set aside for VIPs only.

If he was announcing to all who cared to observe them that *he* was the one who was her escort for the evening then he did not stop to examine why he should be acting so possessively over a woman who had treated him with such disdain. All Pascual knew was that not only did he need to be close to Briana, but he would take a secret sardonic delight in her discomfort too. She had hurt him badly. He knew it was pure animal instinct, but he wanted to find a way of getting back at her for the deed…of ensuring that she would think twice before ever behaving like that again.

Asked what his favourite game was by the club manager, he had no hesitation in replying, 'American Roulette.' Once seated at a circular mahogany table, with a roulette wheel at the centre, and having given their drinks order to a pretty auburn-haired waitress in a short satin lilac dress, he made sure Briana sat next to him on the padded red-velvet seat. His thigh deliberately pressed up against hers. The distinct quiver that shuddered through her made him smile with satisfaction. The sweetly seductive scent of her light perfume and the warmth of her body elicited a similar response inside Pascual. *Dios mio!* He could hardly credit why he should still be so violently attracted to her after all this time.

Something about the combustible mix of chemistry they produced when they were together, obviously.

Seeing the jealous flare in Steve Nichols' pale watchful gaze as he surveyed the brunette with Pascual, the Argentinian ironically found himself musing that all was fair in love and war, and deliberately leaned closer to Briana, so that she gazed up at him with those smoky alluring eyes of hers and coloured hotly.

'You choose the numbers for me tonight,' he instructed softly as the smartly dressed croupier dealt the chips.

'I'm not sure I agree with gambling,' she breathed. 'What if you lose everything because of me?'

As if realising what she had said might also refer to the way their relationship had ended, she let her even white teeth come down hard on her tender lower lip and couldn't hide her intense discomfort.

'I'm sorry,' she murmured.

For a moment Pascual forgot they were in company, in a public albeit supposedly discreet venue that was used to visiting VIPs with a need for privacy, and warred with an almost insatiable urge to savagely claim her mouth and passionately kiss her.

Maybe that could come later? he considered, willing his heartbeat to slow down, unable to tear his heated gaze from hers. A quiet but pervasive excitement took root inside him at the idea.

'Place your bets,' the dealer invited, and Pascual raised an eyebrow at his female companion. 'What will it be?'

Clearly reluctant to participate, but knowing she could hardly refuse, Briana frowned. 'Red six,' she replied.

'Why six?'

'It's always been lucky for me.'

As the little hard white ball hopped and skipped round the moving wheel, every glance round the table seemed hypnotised by it. The other patrons had bet too. Hardly caring whether he won or lost, Pascual felt his heart nearly miss a beat when the ball landed squarely on red six. He had just won thirty-five times his stake, and his had been the only coloured chip on that number.

His hosts and the other two couples round the table politely applauded. When the croupier paid him out in the appropriate chips, he turned and put them on the table in front of Briana.

'Play again,' he urged smoothly, smiling at the shock on her face. 'Perhaps you have other lucky numbers at your disposal? Whatever you win…you keep.'

'I'd rather not, if you don't mind.' Appearing distressed, she pushed to her feet. Her cheeks reddening, she halted a passing cocktail waitress. 'Can you tell me where the ladies' cloakroom is, please?' she asked.

In faint concern, Pascual also got to his feet. He caught Briana's elbow as she started to move away. 'What is the matter? Are you unwell?'

'I shouldn't have come here!' she hissed, her silvery eyes shimmering beneath the twinkling lights of the opulent chandelier sparkling above them. 'I came against my better judgement, and now I wish I hadn't!'

'Why? Are you so averse to winning money?'

'I'm not winning anything, Pascual! It's *your* money that you're so recklessly throwing away to chance, and I want nothing more to do with it.'

'Such principles you have! What a shame they were not in such evidence when you ran away from me in Buenos Aires five years ago, without even giving me a good reason why you'd suddenly decided I was not good enough to be your husband!'

'I saw you kissing another woman!' Jealousy and hurt slashed through Briana's insides like a blade, with no lessening of the pain she had suffered at the time of the incident five years ago.

Remembering where she was, she quickly glanced behind her and realised that they had an audience. She moved her head in anguish. She hadn't meant to just come out with it like that, but the memory had been dragging at her heart from the moment she'd set eyes on Pascual again and she could stem the tide of hurt no longer. Pulling her arm free from his hold, she tried to regain control of her briefly lost equilibrium and restore her dignity.

He considered her with a stunned look. 'Who?' he demanded. 'Who was this woman you saw me kissing?'

'You know very well who!' Her lip trembling, Briana kept her voice low.

'I imagine you are referring to Claudia at the party that night? A very *drunk* Claudia, who barely even knew what she was doing!'

'Oh, she *knew* what she was doing Pascual… And so did you, by the looks of things.'

'Why didn't you tell me you saw this? Was that the real reason you left? *Dios mio!*'

'We'd better not have a scene here, in front of everyone. Think how it will look to your hosts—and it might reflect badly on my business too.'

'Yet you clearly did not care how it looked to my family and friends when you heartlessly deserted me just a week before our wedding!'

Pascual's heart was pounding again, and he almost did not care whether he made a scene or not. The memory of Briana's renunciation of both him and their marriage still cut him to the bone. *And now to discover that she had witnessed that distasteful incident with Claudia, to learn that that was the reason she had left!* Inside he was reeling from the knowledge. Why hadn't she immediately said something to him? Demanded an explanation and given him the chance to tell her that his ex had been drunk and he had frankly been appalled by her throwing herself at him?

Mindful that they were not alone, he had no intention of providing entertainment for the night for all and sundry who might be watching. A more personal discussion of events would have to wait. Giving Briana a stiff little bow, he barely disguised his impatience and annoyance.

'Go to the ladies' cloakroom. When you return I will instruct our driver to take us back to the house. I have suddenly lost my interest in gambling any further tonight!'

* * *

Taking her brush out of her compact leather handbag, Briana made a half-hearted attempt at tidying her hair. The bank of sparkling mirrors in the luxurious ladies' powder room left her with no place to hide her distress. *She should have controlled her emotions better just now in the gaming room!* But it had been so hard, when the reality of Pascual had just kept overwhelming her. And then when he had so carelessly and tauntingly put that little pile of coloured chips in front of her, each one reflecting a sum that would easily pay three months' rent on her house, it had all been too much. Here she was, worrying herself sick over her business and facing potential bankruptcy, and Pascual was acting as if money was nothing to him! But of course with the vast wealth he had at his disposal the value of those coloured chips was even less than a drop in the ocean. If Briana was really honest it was not her financial worries that were causing her the most concern right then. Her little son's beautiful face was constantly in her mind—a face that was a perfect miniature version of his father's—and she wondered how on earth she could break the earth-shattering news of his existence to a man who would probably despise her even more than he did already when he heard it. She had kept Adán from him, and Pascual had every right to deride her.

But she had been utterly devastated when she had seen him with Claudia in his arms that night.

Briana's motives in doing what she had done had only been to try to protect herself and her son from possible future hurt... Not for the first time fear that her decision had been the wrong one clutched deep in her vitals. Claudia had been drunk, he had said. Was he telling her the truth?

Drawing the flat of her hand across her jittery stomach, she resignedly moved away from the un-comfortably candid bank of mirrors and returned to the gaming room. When she did, true to his word Pascual was waiting for her, his dark elegant suit and disturbingly handsome face easily singling him out from all the other men in the room.

'Are you ready to leave?' he asked, his sable eyes flicking over her from head to toe.

'What about the others?' she returned anxiously, glancing back at the roulette table and the three men they had arrived with.

'I will instruct the chauffeur to return for them. Do not fret—we will not leave them stranded!'

Almost complete silence reigned on the journey back to the house. Both parties were painfully, acutely aware of the shattered past that lay between them, and they barely knew how to raise the topic again—a topic that was akin to negotiating a bed of jagged broken glass in their bare feet.

Inevitably, the growing tension gathered uncomfortable strength in the small luxurious space that was the passenger seat of the Rolls…like a small but lethal storm about to break. *There had already been evidence of thunder and lightning.* Thinking back to the scene in the gaming room earlier, when Pascual had let his temper and impatience with her spill over, Briana knew a major confrontation was definitely brewing.

Protectively, she folded her arms over her middle, the too intimate scent of his aftershave and his disturbing body heat unsettling her even more. Everything about the imposing man beside her seemed to emphatically illustrate the marked differences between them. He was wealthy, beautiful and powerful—and as out of reach as he had always been. Oh, he might have professed to love her but he had always held something back…something that had fuelled Briana's already damaging belief that she really *wasn't* quite good enough for him after all. *When she'd seen him kissing his elegant model ex-girlfriend at that tension-filled family party it had inevitably highlighted all her very worst fears that their union wouldn't last— that she wasn't just 'not good enough' but not enough…period!* Now she turned her face away to try and prevent herself from weeping.

Back inside the house, she prayed hard that the confrontation that was definitely imminent would not be tonight. Briana knew she was only putting off the inevitable, but somehow she was feeling far too vulnerable to get into another painful argument with Pascual now—with both of them aiming accusations at each other like lethal missiles and scoring devastating hits. A good night's sleep might help strengthen her besieged resources, so she could face him tomorrow instead.

They were standing at the foot of the impressive Tudor staircase, and she tentatively touched the carved oak handrail, as if to signify her intention to retire. But Pascual's glance was thoughtfully brooding, and it confirmed to her that she would not be allowed to dismiss him or say goodnight as easily as that.

'When I set out from Buenos Aires I had a feeling that something disturbing was going to happen,' he remarked, low-voiced.

As if feeling a chill, Briana rubbed her hands up and down her arms in the thin silk sleeves of her blouse. 'I don't want to ruin your trip, Pascual... honestly, I don't. I know the hurt and resentment you must feel towards me probably still runs deep, but—'

'You are right about that!' His dark eyes flashed, as though his emotions were simmering fire contained behind a mere thin veil. Any moment now the heated sparks would flare into an inferno and incinerate the veil to nothing.

'Look,' she went on, praying he would hear her out and agree, 'tomorrow, after the polo match that's been lined up for you to go to, there'll be time to please yourself what you do next. I'll be here overseeing the arrangements for dinner if you want to come back and talk to me then. I promise I'll give you as long as you like and I won't cut our meeting short. Please, Pascual... It's been a long day and I'm tired tonight.'

'You always *did* manage to get your own way whenever you looked at me like that.'

'Like what?'

'Like a sad, lost little girl.' His lips were twisting wryly, but perhaps with a hint of bitterness in them too, Pascual reached out and touched his fingertips to Briana's soft cheek. 'You could wrap me round your little finger when we were together, and that is the truth!'

'Is it?' Hardly daring to breathe, Briana felt the blood thicken and slow in her veins. There was a tight, coiled feeling in her womb.

'More fool you if you did not know it!' His countenance was unremittingly harsh for a second, but in the next instant it visibly softened and became almost too beguiling for words. Certainly too beguiling for her to resist. 'I will let you go to bed if you give me a kiss,' he intoned huskily. 'For old times' sake.'

Briana was not given time to give Pascual an answer, because suddenly his mouth was on hers, his velvet tongue sliding commandingly between her already partially opened soft lips and dancing with hers in hot, erotic foreplay that heated her blood to fire and stole all the strength from her limbs as though her legs had been violently swept away at the knees.

His hands possessively cupped her hips, impelling them hungrily towards him, and he briefly withdrew his mouth from her lips and suckled the sensitive skin at the side of her neck. When she felt his teeth graze the surface hard enough to sting, Briana gasped out loud. *She was drowning in an erotic sea in which she barely had enough strength left with which to swim.* If she didn't stop this intoxicating insanity right now then she had no doubt she would *not* be spending the night in her room's stately four-poster bed alone.

The thought both shocked and terrified her. As far as she was concerned Pascual Dominguez was a force of nature she could never resist—yet how could she contemplate sleeping with him again when he was not even aware that they had a son together? Her sin, if sin it was, would be compounded way beyond repair.

'You must stop!' Her breathing ragged, she pushed her hands with as much force as she could muster against a chest that was like the hardest steel wall.

'Why?' A silky lock of sable hair flopped sexily across his tanned brow and his expression was mockingly defiant. 'Because you are afraid I will keep you up all night doing all the things I used to do to you that you professed drove you wild, *carino mio*?'

Capturing the handrail for much-needed support, Briana couldn't do one thing about the scarlet flush that she knew seared her face. There wasn't a single inch on her entire body that wasn't burning up with heat at the images Pascual's taunting words so vividly conjured up. When it came to making love, the passion and fire in him had always taken her breath away and made her half crazy with loving him and wanting him, she remembered, aching with sudden renewed longing. But she *had* to be strong!

'I'm here to work...not to provide night-time entertainment for my clients!' she told him indignantly.

'I'm glad to hear it. Because I have no doubt given the chance the admiring Mr Nichols would be at the head of the queue, *amante*!'

Briana shuddered. 'Even if that were true, I can assure you I'm not remotely interested in the man.'

'Good.'

'You don't like him?'

'I have not seen much to make me particularly warm to him as yet,' Pascual confessed candidly. 'This is by no means a done deal, you may be surprised to learn. Like I said before...it is not just about money. I have to be certain that my ponies are going to genuine horse-lovers and will be taken care of as excellently and as well as their pedigree and training dictates they should be.'

'The stables that they own at Windsor certainly have an impressive reputation, so I hear.'

'That may be so... But it is a very recent acquisition for our three businessmen friends, having only lately discovered their passion for polo... That is no guarantee that they know how to run a stable successfully *or* take care of the ponies.'

'Surely there are people there who will know how to do that for them?'

'Even so...' Pascual shrugged. 'But that is enough talk of business for tonight.'

Moving closer, he let his long hands with their surprisingly artistic fingers come to rest either side of Briana's slender upper arms. 'I am sure you are aware that I am much more interested in getting you to agree to spend just one more night with me than in discussing anything else.'

'Why?' Her gaze was steady and direct, even though her heart was racing. 'For old times' sake? Or just to prove you can? Let me save you any doubt if doubt—is what you are suffering from, Pascual. Yes, I still find you attractive, and, yes, I could probably quite easily let you seduce me. But we both know in our hearts it wouldn't be the best of ideas, and it probably wouldn't leave either of us feeling very good. Not physically...but *mentally,* psychologically, I mean. What we had was in the past and, however badly it ended, I really think that that's where it should stay.'

'And leave things as unsatisfactorily unfinished between us as ever?' His expression was scornful. 'That may suit *you*, Briana but it does *not* suit me. I have already had to wait five years to hear from your own lips a full explanation as to why you left, and learning that you saw my ex kissing me at that party is only the tip of the iceberg, I am sure!'

'I promised I would talk to you tomorrow, didn't I?'

'Yes, you did. But, as I am already aware to my detriment that your promises are hardly the *lasting* kind, you can see why I have my doubts.'

Swallowing hard, Briana felt guilt, regret and dread wash through her with equal force. *If her capacity for being honest was in dispute right now, how was Pascual going to react tomorrow when she told him about the son whose existence she had deliberately kept from him?* Her legs felt so weak she wondered how on earth she remained standing.

'Very well.' It seemed he had reluctantly come to a decision. 'We will continue this discussion tomorrow, after I return from the polo match. Now…I am going to go and help myself to a nightcap, then sit in the drawing room for a while and imagine you all alone in your bed to see what fantasies I can conjure up about what you will be wearing. I know you always resisted sleeping naked…is that still the case?'

Remembering how he'd used to tease her about

her 'charming modesty', Briana gripped the stair-rail a little harder as she also recollected that—no matter whether she'd worn something in bed or not—Pascual had always ensured that she ended up naked.

'Goodnight, Pascual,' she murmured, electing to ignore the tantalising question altogether.

'*Buenas noches*, Briana.'

Turning abruptly away with a little half-smile, he made the long walk down the carpeted oak floor to the drawing room. All the while Briana's anxious gaze cleaved to his tall, straight back—until he went inside the door and disappeared from view. The intoxicating taste of him was still clinging to her mouth like some kind of drugging nectar, making her perversely wish for a very different ending to their evening together indeed...

CHAPTER FOUR

IT SOUNDED as if someone was trying to break down the door. Her heart beating like a loud bass drum, Briana let her gaze adjust to the dark for a second, before leaning over to the bedside lamp and switching it on. As soon as light flooded the room she was out of bed in a flash, hurrying to see who her urgent-sounding caller was. Her mind was wild with fear that something unthinkable might have happened to her son.

The figure that loomed up before her out of the semi-darkened corridor was Pascual, and he was glaring at her like a man holding onto the last vestiges of his self-control. His furious, contemptuous gaze seared her to the spot with its ferocity.

'You heartless, selfish little bitch!' he spat out.

'What's wrong?' she asked weakly, her hand nervously going to the V of her short cotton nightie. She was afraid she knew the answer.

Kicking the door shut behind him with the heel of his shoe, he moved towards Briana in head-to-toe black clothing, like some deadly feral panther alighting on his kill, and she honestly thought she might pass out in shock. She was almost tripping over her own feet in her anxious bid to get away, but nonetheless Pascual easily caught her and impelled her towards him, his hard chest acting like an impenetrable wall to confound her escape.

'You have a *son*! A four-year old son! He's mine, isn't he? He *must* be mine! Even *you* would not have deceived me with another man when we were together…not when I made sure that practically every night you were kept occupied in my bed!'

For long, excruciating seconds every possibility of speech deserted Briana. Staring up into the sea of pain and accusation bearing down on her in Pascual's scorching livid gaze, she felt her stomach clench sickeningly with fear and regret.

'How did—?' she began brokenly, hardly even feeling the immovable band of his fingers that was tightly circling her small-boned wrist. 'How did you find out?'

'Your colleague Tina was most illuminating about a lot of things,' he answered scathingly. 'I found her alone in the drawing room, reading, and I suggested she share a nightcap with me. Sitting by a cosy fire, it did not take long for alcohol to loosen her already willing tongue. Before I knew it she was practically telling me your life story!'

'She—she wouldn't!'

Throwing Briana's arm away, as if her touch was nothing less than poison, Pascual snorted. 'How little you seem to know about human nature... No wonder your business is failing! Did you not know that *anyone* can be bought for a price? In your colleague's case just a small sherry was enough for her to spill all your guilty secrets at my feet...like a treasure trove!'

Lost for words for a second time, Briana threaded her fingers through her tousled hair in deepening anguish. If only Tina had not been so free with her conversation, or had made the decision to retire to bed the same time as her boss instead of sitting up to be dazzled by Pascual's undoubted charm! But what troubled her the most was the fact that he had discovered the existence of his son *not* from his mother but from a gossipy colleague! No wonder he was enraged. Nothing would prevent her from taking the full brunt of the blame, even though she still believed she had had good reason to leave him.

'Yes...Adán is your son.' Her mouth was almost too dry to get the words out. Wincing, she lifted her gaze to meet the blistering reply of the man whose sheer charismatic presence seemed to fill up the room, making her feel as if she was relegated to just a small corner of it.

'Adán?' His voice grated, as if he too were having trouble with words. 'You had the temerity to call him by a Spanish name and not even let me—his *father*—know of his existence...why?'

Moving his head from side to side, Pascual couldn't hide his torment and Briana's heart went out to him—even though she knew he would likely despise and detest any compassion she demonstrated.

'Why did I give him a Spanish name?'

'No! Why did you keep the fact that you were pregnant from me and disregard my feelings as though they were of no account whatsoever? I thought that you could not hurt me any worse than you did when you left...without giving me even the smallest indication that you were planning such an unbelievable act. But now I have discovered that you are capable of *far* worse crimes. I was wrong to think that I knew you, Briana... Your behaviour is beyond my understanding and makes you an utter stranger to me!'

Staring at her, Pascual saw a myriad of emotions cross her pale just-stirred-from-sleep face. But he wished he could see *more* than just the evidence of feelings there. He wished he had a mental microscope to probe deep inside her heart and see if he could understand what had motivated her to deal him such a cruel and yet perversely *wondrous* blow all at the same time?

The news that he was a father had turned his

whole world upside down, and it was by far the most momentous thing he had ever heard. But right now rage and despair were the prevalent emotions crashing through him, battering him like a violent cyclone at the thought that he had already missed out on four years of his child's life because of the woman that stood in front of him.

Had he somehow treated her so badly that she would act in such a vicious way towards him? He did not think so. From the first he had always treated her with the utmost care and respect...*hadn't he?* Because of the immense gravity of what she'd done to him, there was a painful glimmer of doubt in Pascual's mind. Had he missed out something important? Searching his memory with rapier-like honesty, he could recall nothing that he'd done or said to wound her in any way. Apart from that unfortunate scene at the party that his inebriated ex had instigated *the incident which he had tried to explain had been genuinely nothing to do with him...* No, he concluded. That could not be the *only* reason she had kept him in the dark about his child. This was all about what had been going on with Briana personally, and he vowed he would let nothing stand in the way of his getting to the bottom of it.

Looking distressed, she brushed back her hair with a trembling hand, and Pascual's attention was helplessly drawn to the short pastel blue night garment she wore that resembled an oversized T-shirt—probably a chainstore item that had not been designed to be alluring in any way, he guessed. Her lack of sophistication and guile-free attitude towards things like that had once totally charmed him. And even now, in the midst of his disbelief and despair at what she had done, his libido was unequivocally and treacherously aroused by the sight of her body in the plain, nondescript nightwear...the firm rounded breasts that pressed against the thin material, nipples provocatively erect, the perfect Botticelli angel-like curve of her hips and her long shapely bare thighs.

'I've anguished so long about talking to you about things. Then it turned out you're the VIP guest this weekend and—and it was such a shock. I wasn't deliberately trying to avoid discussing what happened between us earlier... I just needed time to get my bearings.'

'So now you have had *plenty* of time to deal with the fact that I am here—and you owe me an explanation...to put it mildly!'

'Why don't you sit down?' Moving gracefully towards the striped pink and cream slipper chair that she'd laid her robe across, she gathered up the flimsy blue garment and slipped it on over the matching oversized T-shirt, leaving the chair empty.

Barely knowing how to contain his impatience and frustration at what he perceived to be deliberate delaying tactics, Pascual threw up his hands in temper. 'Do not tell me what to do!' A string of Spanish invective escaped him, and he saw the frisson of fear that flickered across the darkened grey irises, but just then he refused to concern himself with the fact she might be intimidated by him. 'All I want is a truthful explanation of your actions. After that...'

'After that...what?'

'*Dios mio!* Just stop wasting time and *tell* me!'

'All right. I—I wanted to tell you not long after you'd proposed... There's no easy way to soften this, but the truth is I'd begun to seriously realise that I was only kidding myself that a marriage between us could ever work.'

The sense of rejection and pain that had never left him since Briana had walked out coiled like a band of steel round Pascual's chest and squeezed as tight as a deadly cobra, intent on crushing it.

'You only have to start with our backgrounds,' she continued, unable to disguise her apprehension. 'You were born into the most extraordinary wealth and privilege, with all the expectations that go along with that, and I came from much more... shall we say ordinary beginnings? I was never going to fit into the incredibly elite lifestyle you were used to, Pascual! Your family made me quite aware of that very early on. They saw me as a drifter. Someone with no purpose or direction because I had taken time off from my usual routine to travel and work at not very prestigious jobs to keep myself.'

'Why bring my family into this? You are just using them as a convenient excuse. You clearly did not feel the same way for me as I felt for you, and were simply too cowardly to just come out and say it!'

'No! That's not how it was at all.'

'Then why did you not tell me that you were pregnant? How could you have left, knowing that you were carrying my baby? What kind of man do you think I am that I would not be interested in such an incredible piece of information? Did you not think that I would want to know my *own* child and have some say in how he was raised? You must either have taken temporary leave of your senses or you are even more heartless than I thought!'

The lovely face before him crumpled a little, but quickly she appeared to gather herself and determinedly returned her gaze to Pascual's. As he studied her, his heart was thundering as fast as a racehorse galloping for the finishing line. Years of turmoil and anguish over her desertion had just reached a crescendo, and he had no intention of reigning in his emotions now. *Especially* since he had so shockingly discovered that Briana had had his baby and had deliberately kept him in ignorance of the fact.

She pressed her hand to her chest. 'I didn't *know*

I was pregnant when I left. I only found out a couple of weeks after I got home… The thing is, Pascual…'

For a moment the depth of pain that glimmered in her ethereal grey eyes and the small catch in her voice unexpectedly got through the armour he had erected and pierced him.

'This is the truth. I had personal experience of what it was like, coming from parents from two different worlds, and it made for a very schizophrenic upbringing…a painful one too. My mother was from an ordinary working class background but my father went to public school and when they met was training to be a barrister. Unlike you and I—' heated colour swept into her face '—they *did* marry… But somehow their initial strong attraction for each other couldn't bridge the social and educational divide between them and the relationship quickly got into trouble. They rowed a lot, and my mum says that my father started to put her down by making fun of where she'd come from and her lack of education. But even when he was cruel to her she still loved him, she said. Then he went and made things even worse by having an affair…the first of many.'

Pushing some of her tousled hair away from her flushed cheek, Briana gazed into the distance for a moment, clearly haunted by what had happened.

'When I was just five years old they broke up. I grew up spending two weekends a month with my father, in his ancestral family home in Dorset, and the rest of the time with my mother in a tiny mid-terrace house in Camberwell. When I was with my father he got his housekeeper to take care of me. He used to call me his "regrettable mistake". After the divorce he quickly remarried…someone from his *own* class. None of his family ever welcomed me or made me feel at home, and after every painful visit I couldn't wait to get back to my mum's! We no longer keep in touch, in case you're wondering.'

A heavy sigh fell on the air.

'When I met you, Pascual, I really wanted to believe that where we both came from wouldn't sabotage our future together. But then I started to have the most terrible doubts…doubts that just wouldn't go away. The dinner parties and polo matches you took me to with your wealthy friends, the disdain I saw in your family's eyes because I was not from the same background… Well…it finally got to me. And because of the way I'd seen things play out between my own parents I knew I was only kidding myself that our relationship could work. Then I saw you with your ex that night, and suddenly I knew the hell my mother must have gone through when the man she loved had an affair. I knew then that I could never be with someone who might have the capacity to be unfaithful…that it would likely destroy me.'

'*Dios mio!* I *told* you what really happened!' Pascual interjected with frustration. 'She had had too much to drink—the woman was just making mischief. She was jealous because it was you I wanted to marry and not her. I thought I showed you in so many ways that I genuinely loved you and wanted no other. And yet you judged me so quickly over that stupid incident, and did not even give me the chance to defend myself before you chose to walk out!'

'I saw what I saw and I was devastated. Given my background, surely you can understand that now? I just couldn't take the risk that once we were married you might quickly grow tired of me and have affairs. You see, I didn't want what we had to turn into something ugly and painful. Nor did I want to be someone else's regrettable mistake either! As for Adán... When I found myself pregnant with him, I anguished for a long time about what to do for the best. Obviously I had to make some decisions about his future. I found myself asking how, in all practicality, he could go to and from Argentina every month to visit you. The situation would have been impossible. All a parent wants for their child is for them to grow up feeling loved and secure, and I finally came to the conclusion that I could only do that for him if he stayed with me. In the cold light of day I know it sounds utterly despicable to have made that decision without involving you. But, having walked out on you, I simply *had* to make it.'

'You keep referring to the child as *your* baby, but *I* had a part in making him too—did I not?' Emotion locked inside Pascual's throat and he struggled to speak past it. 'Why did you not tell me all this about your background before? You should never have just left without speaking to me first. To have a note thrust into my hand the day after a party that had been meant to celebrate our upcoming marriage and read that you had left was unbelievable. I thought I was having a nightmare!'

Staring briefly down at the floor, Pascual recalled the devastation that had for a time driven him to the very pits of despair and shook his head.

'I—it was hard to think straight at the time,' said Briana. 'Preparations were going ahead for the wedding, and every day I got more and more scared that I was making a dreadful mistake… Then that incident with your ex happened.'

'And you could not talk to me about any of these things? I was not some uncaring stranger…I was supposedly the man that you loved!'

'You *were*! I mean, you—'

His glance was withering. 'I fear your explanations have come far too late, *carino mio*. You should know that nothing you can say to me now could ever regain you my trust or respect. Any feelings I might once have had for you have been crushed to dust by what you have done!'

Moving across the room, Pascual tried hard to clear his head. The rain outside thudded with force against the old-fashioned leaded windowpanes, echoing the sensation of pressure building up inside him. So many thoughts, regrets and painful feelings were crowding his mind and his heart that he almost could not stand it. But out of all the turmoil, one thought gripped him more than any other. *He had a son.*

Recalling how passionately his friend Fidel had felt about *his* only son, he was deluged by the strongest determination to make things right in that quarter at least. He might have not been present in the first four years of his child's life, but by God he would be *more* than present in the rest of it!

Turning back to survey the lone slender figure standing in the centre of the room, he ruthlessly stamped out any fleeting feelings of sympathy that arose inside him. It was true what he had told Briana…her explanations *had* come too late. *Whatever happened next…she had brought it all upon herself.*

'I do not want to discuss this any further tonight. I need time to think. It has come as the greatest shock to me to learn what I have learned…that I have a son. A son whose *cold* and selfish mother decided that I did not have the *right* to know about him! We will talk again tomorrow, after the polo match… By which time I will have come to some important decisions where both you and he are concerned.'

'Any decisions about the future are not just up to you, Pascual!'

'If I were you, Briana,' he said, his furious glance utterly scathing, 'I would not risk saying anything more on that subject tonight. You have already had everything your way for far too long. You should know that I do not intend to let that situation continue...*believe* me.'

Striding to the door, realising that a serious explosion of temper was imminent if he stayed in the same room with her for even a second longer, Pascual let himself out into the narrow dimly lit corridor and did not look back...

'Rough night?' Tina's relentlessly cheerful tone almost made Briana snap when she joined her for breakfast in the kitchen the next morning. Her nerves were on edge as she poured herself coffee from the generous-sized cafetière on the ornate sideboard, and she threw the other woman a wry glance. 'You could say that.'

Carrying her cup across to the sturdy oak table, she pulled out a chair and sat down. Reaching for the milk jug and sugar bowl, she absently added some of the contents of each to her drink. It was clear the dark shadows beneath her eyes must reveal she'd hardly slept a wink—but what woman could possibly sleep after that distressingly painful scene when Pascual had woken her from sleep in the middle of the night? And exactly *what* important decisions had he reached about her and Adán after he had left her? she wondered anxiously.

Last night he had been *beyond* furious, and a big part of her acknowledged that she deserved his condemnation. She should never have kept Adán a secret from him, no matter how scared she was of her future life repeating her mother's. The tragedy was that she had loved this man so much—with all her being, in fact—and seeing him again she had shockingly realised that her love had not died. It had merely been lying dormant.

There had been a few moments during their unhappy confrontation last night when Briana had wanted to reach out to Pascual and beg his forgiveness…to ask him how she could start to make amends. But so fearful was she of what he might demand that she hadn't been able to bring herself to do it. Now she anguished over whether he might seriously contest her for custody of their son, and the icy tentacles of fear that were running in the back of her mind and in the pit of her stomach clutched at her even more. With his incredible wealth and powerful family Pascual had all the means necessary to take Adán from her, and there would be *nothing* Briana could do about it. In the light of this most worrying crisis of all going to court for an outstanding business debt couldn't be *less* important!

Hardly knowing what to do about anything right then, she gazed despondently into the beverage, watching the curling wisps of steam from the delicate porcelain cup in front of her as if she was staring into a dark tunnel with little prospect of ever finding a source of light at the end. If only her father had not been so incapable of staying faithful to her mother— had put her and his daughter's welfare above the snob value of class and money he had grown up with—then maybe Briana wouldn't have found herself in the heart-rending situation she was in now with Pascual.

'What's the matter, Bri?'

As she dropped down into the seat opposite, there was genuine concern on Tina's pretty face. Mindful of what the girl had unknowingly revealed to Pascual last night, Briana felt naturally reluctant to discuss anything personal. Her young colleague hadn't meant any harm, she was sure, but she shouldn't have been quite so free with her conversation.

'I'm fine. I just didn't sleep very well, that's all.'

'Our gorgeous Mr Dominguez was asking me about you last night. In fact every time I tried to turn the conversation around to something else he turned it back to you! I think he really likes you, Bri.'

'It's neither here nor there whether the man likes me or not. I'm just here to do my job and that's all. And in future I'd be very grateful if you wouldn't tell all and sundry about my personal circumstances. *Especially* not people I've been hired to work for.'

Appearing genuinely shocked at her boss's uncharacteristic burst of temper, Tina shrugged apologetically. 'I'm really sorry. It was just that he was being so charming, and before I knew it he'd got things out of me that I normally wouldn't tell anyone under pain of death! About the business being in difficulty, I mean, and you being a single mum…'

'I accept your apology. But trust me…if you want to get on in this business as well as in life, Tina, you need to learn to be a lot more discreet! Now, I'm going to finish my coffee and then we've both got things to get on with. And if Mr Dominguez asks you any more questions about me just tell him to come and ask me himself, will you?'

CHAPTER FIVE

HE'D sat up nearly all night mulling over events, thinking what to do. Finally, needing some air, he walked out of the still sleeping house and headed off—hands deep in the pockets of his trenchcoat—down one of the winding country lanes that led away from the house. Dawn was just breaking, and a silvery mist was draped over the trees and hedgerows like a diaphanous cloak. The air contained just enough frost in it to make Pascual shiver. The English countryside in the autumn was a sight to stir the heart, he silently acknowledged, his shoes flattening damp golden leaves deep into the gravelled lane as he walked, and he experienced the first real pleasure he had had since arriving.

Back home in Buenos Aires the temperature would be a predictable twenty-two degrees, warm and sunny. But strangely at that moment he felt no particular longing for the place of his birth. Where he was right now was perfect because that was where his son was, he realized—that was enough to make Pascual content to be there. *What did he look like, this boy of his?* Did any of his features resemble his father's? What characteristics might they share? Feeling his throat tighten almost unbearably, he muttered something impatient into the frigid air.

How could she have done it? How could Briana have deliberately kept his child from him? Even if he had cheated on her with Claudia—which he most definitely had *not*—was he deserving of such unbelievable treatment? And just because her faithless father had had affairs, did it naturally follow that Pascual would do the same? He was a different kind of man entirely…an honourable, *loyal* man. If only she had seen that. And he was even less likely to have an affair knowing he had a child to think of! How was it possible that he had once loved such an untrusting woman—a woman who had preferred to leave him rather than stay and hear his side of the story?

Preferring to focus on solutions rather than regrets, and for the moment determinedly putting the past aside, he concentrated on some of the decisions he'd reached last night about the future. *When he returned to Buenos Aires in a couple of days he would be taking the boy back with him.* No question about it. 'When you become a father,' his friend Fidel had once told him, 'everything changes. In a way the path becomes much clearer. You are less concerned with your own needs and ambitions. Instead almost every waking moment is given over to this precious child you have helped bring into the world...'

Sadly, his friend had not lived to see his own child grow up. Having already missed out on Adán's infant years, Pascual was determined that from now on it would be a very different story for *him*. And if Briana made it difficult in any way, then he would not hesitate to take a legal route to claiming what was his. *But he hoped it would not come to that.* Much better that she saw she had done both him and his son a grave injustice in keeping them apart, was ready to right a wrong rather than make that wrong even worse by obstructing him.

Taking a moment to expel a long, troubled breath, he continued on his journey up the winding lane. He almost stumbled when he remembered the kiss he had stolen last night—*before* he had found out about his son. Heat coiled in his belly with a fierce demand that shocked him. *How could it be that she could still arouse such lust and need in him even after five years of being apart?* Feeling betrayed by his own body, Pascual impatiently lengthened his stride. He would walk hard for a while and burn up some of the nervous heightened energy that throbbed through him, he concluded grimly. His treacherous and inconvenient desire would give him no peace if he did not.

And there was something else he had made a decision about. The planned visit to a polo match at one of Britain's most elite sports grounds today no longer held any appeal for him, he realised—end of the season or no. No... He had far more important upcoming events commanding his thoughts—the first one entailed putting Briana in the picture about his plans, and the next was visiting his son...

Dumbfounded, Briana stared at her fresh-faced colleague. 'What do you mean he's decided not to go to the polo match? The others are all waiting outside in the car for him! What reason did he give you?'

Looking uncomfortable, as well as bewildered, Tina frowned. 'He just said that he'd changed his mind...that something more important had come up and to send his apologies. He'll meet the others at dinner tonight, he said. In the meantime...'

The younger girl hesitated, and Briana's heartbeat quickened with apprehension. 'In the meantime...what?' she demanded, fear making her tone impatient.

'In the meantime Mr Dominguez said he'd like to talk to you in private...in his room.'

The blonde's curious glance spoke volumes, and inwardly Briana groaned. That was *all* she needed. Tina speculating that there was something going on between the gorgeous Argentinian and her boss!

Then she remembered the slightly pink abrasion at the side of her neck—the parting gift that Pascual had left her with last evening—and her face and body briefly burned with self-conscious and guilty heat. Automatically she lifted her hand to tug the silk collar of her blouse closer to the skin there.

'Well, then…you'll have to go outside and repeat what you've just told me to our clients… Needless to say *not* the part about Pas—Mr Dominguez wanting to see me in his room!'

Feeling her face flame at inadvertently almost exposing herself even more, Briana turned abruptly away and reluctantly—feeling as though she had *lead* in her shoes—ascended the staircase to the landing where Pascual's suite was situated.

Nibbling worriedly on her lip, she rapped smartly on the oak door.

'Come in!'

Giving her a briefly cold look, his sensual mouth bracketed by distinct displeasure, Pascual held the door wide to invite her in. Clothed from head to toe in stylish black once again, his indomitable maleness projected the arresting package of a man used to giving orders and being in charge—and heaven help anyone who dared to obstruct him.

Briana's anxiety went up several notches merely at the intimidating sight of him. Closing the door behind them, he followed her into the centre of the room. The maid had put fresh flowers into a huge white vase on the polished chiffonier, and the scent of lilies in particular lay on the air like an exotic and drugging perfume. It only took one glance into the disturbing midnight gaze before her and she knew she was in trouble.

Just the same she ventured, 'Why—why don't you want to go to the polo match?'

'Because my priorities have changed…as I am sure you are well aware.'

Saying nothing in return, she sensed the atmosphere spark as dangerously as a flickering flame near a bale of straw.

'You may well be silent!' A muscle jerked briefly in the shadowed hard jaw. 'Because I warn you that nothing you can say can alter the path I have resolved to take. When I leave for Buenos Aires in two days' time you and my son are coming with me for an extended holiday—a holiday during which time a marriage between us will take place. The marriage that should have taken place five years ago!'

'What?'

'You heard me. And when you return to the UK it will only be for the purposes of winding up your business and closing it down.'

'Closing it down?'

'Sí. It is in trouble anyway, is it not? It can only be a relief to put it behind you. Once you are back in

Buenos Aires, instead of running a business you will have to get used to fulfilling the role of my wife instead. Do not worry, Briana…' Pascual's dark-eyed gleam was deliberately provocative '…there will be plenty to keep you occupied as far as *that* position is concerned. And that includes sharing my bed, mothering our son, playing hostess at any dinner parties I may give and being my *unimpeachable* escort at any social functions we may attend as I attempt to integrate you into my world. The world you clearly despise so much you could not bear to entertain being a part of it! You can quickly forget any ideas you may have had about remaining a single mother and raising our child on your own in England. That was in the past. Today is a new day, and from now on things are going to look very different for you. You can count on it!'

Feeling as if a storm had just ripped off the roof of her house, Briana found the power of speech had temporarily eluded her. It was as though what she'd just heard had rendered her mute with shock.

'Have you nothing to say?' Pascual thrust his implacable jaw forward in annoyance.

'Yes…I do.' Her returning glance was wary. 'I have plenty to say. But whether you'll listen to it or not is another thing.'

'I will listen. It does not mean that I will concur or change my mind.'

'I understand that you want to be in Adán's life,

and that is your right as his father. But you can't really be serious about us going back to Buenos Aires with you and the two of us getting married. We surely don't have to go *that* far? And anyway…I can't believe that you'd even *want* to marry me after what's happened between us. It just doesn't make any sense.'

He scowled. 'Well, it is certainly not because I have found I cannot live without you, or anything as ludicrous as that! No. I am doing this purely for the benefit of my son. The son you have denied me for the past four years. You are his mother, and even though you have not shown me the least respect in any way I will accord *you* respect and not let him down. No…I intend to become the father to Adán that I should have been right from the beginning—and if that entails marrying his treacherous mother, then—'

'Treacherous?' Briana's grey eyes rounded in protest. 'I never cheated on you…*ever*! If anyone showed any tendency to be attracted to other people, it was you!'

'You are still holding a grudge about that ridiculous scene with Claudia?' Pascual sighed with impatience. 'What can I say that will convince you of the truth? I swear to you that she was drunk. Because I had broken up with her and she was mad at me, she wanted to make me look bad in front of you. I had not even realised you saw what happened! If I had you can be sure I would have talked to you about it and explained. But you never gave me the chance to do that, did you?'

'I was too upset and shocked!'

'And apparently you believed that I was just like your father! The reason I call you treacherous is that you made me a promise that you would become my wife, Briana. You did not keep that promise. Instead you left and made me look like a fool in front of everyone I cared about, and then kept the fact that you were pregnant with my son a secret up until now. Disloyal, duplicitous, untrustworthy… Treacherous is as good a word as any in your English vocabulary to describe your actions…would you not agree?'

'Even if you think that, you can't really expect me to go along with your plans without protest and simply do everything you command, Pascual. We're not living in the Middle Ages, here, and I'm not going to agree with everything you say simply because I feel bad about what happened between us five years ago!'

'So you feel bad, do you? At last! Some indication of regret!'

'Of course I feel bad about what happened. Every day…watching Adán grow…I've thought about what he's missing by not having his father in his life. I truly regret what I did as regards to that. But I wasn't being vindictive or cruel by not contacting you about him. At the time…considering the strain I was under…I just did what I thought was right.'

'It is my view that you did not employ any *thinking* at all in the matter! You purely reacted! I knew you could be impulsive and I liked that about you…but I did not guess in a million years that that impulsive nature of yours would lead you to take the drastic steps that you took five years ago.' His blistering glance narrowed. 'I have a question. Did you *ever* plan to contact me about Adán at all? What if business had *not* brought me to the UK this week? What if you had *not* been providing hospitality services at the same venue where my meeting was being held? Would you have let more time go by? Perhaps not getting in touch until our son was a grown man? Maybe not even then?'

It was a terrible thought. And one that made Briana feel as if she had committed a crime that carried a life sentence. It was not the first time that the gravity of the decision she'd made in leaving Buenos Aires five years ago hit her so hard. But never before had it swept over her leaving such destroying hurt and regret in its wake. Faced with the flesh-and-blood reality of the handsome, vital man in front of her, she began to see exactly what she had done to him. Because of her he had suffered humiliation and torment—and he was suffering doubly now. Instead of going through with the marriage and committing herself to the man she had truly loved she had let fear and doubt rule the day—and this scene that was akin to torture was the result.

Again she wished that she'd had a better example of a man than her deceitful, cruel father... Whatever way she reflected on it, her actions had resulted in denying Pascual the opportunity of having a relationship with his own son. Even if he potentially *might* have strayed in their marriage—and Briana had to recall the devastation she had endured when she'd seen him in the arms of his ex in Buenos Aires and believed the worst—he surely didn't deserve that? Breathing out a troubled breath, she moved a few paces towards him. With all her heart she wished she knew a way to make everything right again, but she realised that was like wishing she could turn back time. It was simply beyond human capability.

'You were always there at the back of my mind, Pascual. I suppose I just got caught up in the day-to-day demands of trying to run a business and support myself and Adán,' she explained. 'And because so much time had gone by without us speaking I worried that if I *did* contact you, you'd either slam down the phone or...if I went to Buenos Aires...shut the door in my face!'

'Knowing that I had a son? You really believed I would do that?' With even more disbelief, Pascual dropped his hands to the lean, masculine hips encased in black corded trousers. 'It makes me realise even more that you do not know what kind of man I am Briana. Words desert me at the idea that you thought I would not be interested in the fact that I had fathered a son with you!'

Disturbed by the thought that clearly she *hadn't* really known Pascual as well as she'd thought she had, and feeling a sense of shame wash over her, Briana lifted her shoulders uneasily. 'What can I do to help make things right?'

Levelling his black velvet gaze right at her, Pascual did not hesitate to illustrate. 'Apart from doing as I outlined and coming back to Buenos Aires with me? You can arrange for a car to drive us to where you live so that I may at last become acquainted with my son!'

'But that's three hours away and another three back... You won't make dinner tonight with our clients if we do that.'

When she saw how Pascual received *that* particular piece of information, Briana instantly regretted speaking her thoughts out loud. But she hadn't *only* been thinking of what her clients would say if he did not meet them for dinner as arranged. She was genuinely concerned for her son, and how he would cope if she suddenly arrived home with a man he'd never seen before and declared that he was his father!

'Do you think I *care* about attending a business dinner over seeing my child for the first time?' Pascual uttered furiously. 'Tell them I will meet them in London tomorrow instead...they can name the venue. You can say that something of the utmost importance has called me away. Why not?' The formidably broad shoulders beneath the perfectly fitted black shirt lifted in a dismissive shrug. 'It is the truth.'

'First I'll have to ring my mother to tell her we're coming. She's been looking after Adán for me while I've been away this weekend.'

'Do that—and then arrange for a car. I am anxious to get going as soon as possible.'

'I have my own car here. I can drive us.'

'Good. Then go and make your phone call and let us not waste any more time, hmm?'

Clearly dismissing her, Pascual turned away to reach for the water jug and glass on the coffee table to pour a drink. Feeling as if her limbs had turned as fluid as the water in the jug, Briana moved towards the door and silently exited the room.

Once outside, in the monastic quiet of the corridor, she briefly leant against the panelled wall, trying hard to stem the sudden onrush of fear and doubt that had overtaken her about the impending visit home. *How would it be*, she wondered, *when father and son came face to face for the very first time?* Her little son could be shy and uncommunicative even with people he knew—let alone strangers. How would Pascual react if his child appeared to reject him?

Feeling for them both, she felt hot tears well helplessly behind her eyes and spill over onto her cheeks.

Impatiently scrubbing at them with the heel of her hand, she pushed away from the wall and returned to her room to make the phone call…

The house was situated down a pleasant tree-lined street in one of London's less busy boroughs. It was a neat terraced property, painted white, and next to the other less bright edifices on either side of it easily stood out. As Pascual followed a definitely subdued Briana up the short path that led to the front door, with its pretty stained glass panelling, adrenaline shot through him like rapids at the prospect of meeting his little son.

He'd quizzed her on the way about him, but she'd seemed almost reluctant to give him answers—just as if she was preserving the right to hold onto that information…as if she feared that if Pascual knew too much he would make it even harder for her to keep the boy to herself. It infuriated him that Briana was still reluctant to let him into their lives when all he wanted was the chance to be a proper father. *Every bit of trust between them was gone.* It had all been smashed into the dirt five years ago. And now they stood on either side of the ground they were both determined to capture—like warring factions in a soul-destroying battle instead of the passionate lovers they had once been.

As Briana let herself into the narrow hallway with

her key, along with his great anticipation at meeting his son Pascual sensed the full extent of her betrayal of his heart as he had never sensed it before—and right then his soul had never felt bleaker...

CHAPTER SIX

HER mother was the first person to greet them. Her usually calm and attractive features looking strained, Frances Douglas glanced behind her daughter at the tall, startlingly good-looking man behind her and frowned. When Briana had told her that she was unexpectedly returning home early, and bringing Adán's father back with her to visit, her ensuing soft intake of breath had spoken volumes.

Whilst knowing that her mother wouldn't unfairly judge any decision she made—and indeed had *never* judged her for leaving Buenos Aires so abruptly, calling off her planned marriage and returning home pregnant—Briana realised that this impromptu visit by Pascual would naturally fill her with anxiety about her daughter and grandson's future…as it did Briana herself. But right this minute her heart was thumping like a full-blown percussion band inside her chest at the knowledge that Adán might run out into the hallway at any moment to set eyes on his father for the very first time…

'Hi, Mum.' Her gaze was quizzical as she kissed the older woman's scented, powdered cheek. 'Where's Adán?'

'Asleep on the couch. I took him swimming. They had all the inflatable toys out in the pool, and he was tired by the time I got him home. He's been out for the count for about half an hour or so.' Warily, Frances glanced up at the dark-haired Adonis who was currently making Briana's tiny hallway resemble the entrance to a doll's house instead of a normal-sized dwelling. 'I presume this must be—'

'Pascual Dominguez.' Standing aside to make the awkward introductions, Briana somehow made her lips form a smile. 'Adán's father. Pascual—this is my mother, Frances.'

Catching the instantly disturbing drift of his expensive cologne as he extended his hand past her to greet her mother, Briana sensed his disapproval of her informality.

Her intuition was proved right when he announced, 'Mrs Douglas…it is good to meet you at last.'

'As I'm sure you heard me tell Briana just now,' her mother replied, 'Adán is asleep and may not stir for a while.'

'It does not matter. I have waited a long time already to see my son. I will wait as long as I have to until he wakes.' This time Pascual made no bones about casting his meaningful gaze at Briana directly, so that she couldn't mistake his displeasure with her.

'Well...shall we go into the living room, then? That's where he'll be if he's asleep on the couch.'

'And in the meantime...shall I make some tea for us all?' Frances suggested, her even-voiced tone acting as temporary balm to the tension that had enveloped them all.

'A cup of coffee would be most welcome...black, no sugar...*gracias*.'

'And you, darling?' Briana's mother started to move towards the long galley kitchen at the end of the hallway, with its cheerful red and white checked curtains.

Hardly able to think straight for the emotion that was tightening her chest, Briana answered distractedly. 'Tea would be great—thanks.'

'After you.' Observing her glance towards the living room door, Pascual gestured that she precede him.

In the small square room with its pine bookshelves crammed with books and CDs, its small television, compact music system and carpeted floor strewn with various children's toys, her small son was lying asleep on the smaller of the two dark gold couches. His slumbering form was covered warmly with a cheerful patchwork rug Briana had made last winter. On the pillow his curly dark hair framed a sweetly heart-shaped face that wouldn't shame an angel, she thought lovingly, her heart constricting with a surge of strong emotion as she gazed down at him.

Sensing Pascual move next to her, she glanced up, her pulse racing hard at the realisation that his handsome face was equally affected. He was moved by what he saw. Adán was an exceptionally beautiful child, and people often stopped her in the street to tell her so. *But then how could he not be beautiful when he had a father who looked like Pascual?* Briana concluded.

Straight away she knew that he could see that the boy was his. At least there would be no degrading speculation about paternity to deal with, on top of all the other accusations that he'd levelled her way, she mused with relief.

'He looks not unlike myself as a small boy,' he commented quietly beside her, the warmth in his voice replacing its previous chill.

'He's often mistaken for a girl with those lustrous curls!' Briana smiled back. 'But I can't bring myself to cut his hair short yet.'

'My mother would feel the same if she saw him. She had the same dilemma with me.'

'Did she?'

Almost afraid to say anything, in case she broke the suddenly intimate spell that seemed to enfold them, Briana crossed her arms over her silk shirt and

chewed apprehensively down on her lip. She remembered Paloma Dominguez well. The woman was as
tall and striking-looking as her son, and could be
equally intimidating. Once upon a time she had been
one of the world's most famous fashion models. It
was hard to imagine her as a relaxed young mum,
making a fuss of her beautiful little boy…

'How long will he sleep, do you think?' Crouching
down beside the couch, Pascual leaned forward to
brush back some of the wayward silky curls from the
child's creamy smooth forehead.

Watching, Briana almost held her breath. Knowing from experience how tender as well as passionate this man's touch could be, she knew a spon-
taneous longing for him to touch *her* as gently and
reverently. All the things she had loved about him
were coming back to her in a beguiling wave of
powerful memory, and every defence was suddenly
terrifyingly open and vulnerable to him. Seeing him
with their child, Briana felt even more exposed.

'He should wake very soon. He'll be hungry,'
she answered.

Rising to his feet, Pascual studied her deeply.
'How could you have kept him from me?'

Her gaze locked with the heartbreak in his un-
guarded ebony eyes, and regret and sadness almost
made her stumble. 'I see now that it was wrong of
me,' she said, her voice dropping to almost a whisper.

'Yes…it *was*. Whatever you think I did to you…I did *not* deserve this!'

'Mummy?'

At that very moment Adán stirred, and both adults' attention was immediately diverted.

Hurriedly wiping at her moist eyes, Briana dropped down onto the edge of the couch and drew the small sleepy form into her arms. 'Hello, my angel. Grandma told me she took you swimming… did you have a lovely time?'

'Yes…' Adán's voice was still husky from sleep. He leant his curly dark head against his mother's chest, then glanced up warily at the tall dark man looking down at him.

Bestowing a kiss at the side of his soft cheek, Briana tightened her arms a little round his pliant warm frame. 'Sweetheart…I've brought someone home to meet you. His name is Pascual, and he's—'

'A friend.'

To her complete surprise, Pascual dropped down onto his haunches and took one of Adán's small chubby hands in his own. 'I have heard a lot about you from your mother, Adán and I have been looking forward so much to meeting you. I hope you do not mind?'

Her heartbeat regaining a more normal cadence, Briana threw him a grateful glance. His sensitivity in not immediately declaring who he was to their son completely took her aback, and she gazed at him as if confirming what he had said a while ago—she *hadn't* really known him at all, all those years ago. Instead she'd allowed her fears of being rejected to consume her and colour her judgement of him completely.

To her surprise, Adán was smiling at Pascual as if he was far from a stranger, and he was struggling to sit up straight so that he could more easily talk to the man who still held his hand in his. 'I've got lots of cars!' he declared. 'Would you like to see them?'

'Of course. I would *love* to see them.'

Smiling, Pascual quickly stood up, moving swiftly to the side as the small whirlwind on Briana's lap jettisoned itself off the couch and flew across the room to drop down beside a large blue plastic box in front of the television. Several small model cars were plunked onto the floor and pushed towards Pascual as Adán retrieved them one by one from the box.

'Look!' he said, eyes shining. 'I've got a Ferrari!'

'I've got one of those too.' His face perfectly serious as he knelt beside him on the carpet, Pascual held up the toy car to examine it interestedly.

'What colour?' Adán demanded.

'Silver.'

'I like this black one best.'

'You are right. It is a much better colour than silver.' Adán beamed.

Briana's mother returned with the tea and coffee. As she straightened from leaving the tray on a small side-table, she glanced pointedly at her daughter. 'Is everything all right, darling? Do you want me to stay, or shall I leave you all alone for a while?'

Now she glanced over at Pascual, seated on the floor with her small grandson. He looked as at home with him as if he'd been a father to the boy from day one.

Gazing back at her, Pascual formed his lips into the most disarming of smiles. 'Do not worry, Mrs Douglas...I am only here visiting with Adán. I do not intend to make a scene...you have my word on that.'

'She's done a good job in raising him...you'll soon find that out.' An emotional catch in her voice, Frances quickly withdrew her glance from Pascual's and returned it to Briana. 'Are you staying here tonight, or do you have to go back?'

'We are going back,' Pascual said clearly. The expression in his eyes was hard to decipher, momentarily duelling with Briana's. 'Unfortunately I have one more meeting that I need to attend. But I will come and see Adán again tomorrow.'

'Do you mind staying over with Adán tonight, as planned?' Briana asked, her mind whirling at the implications of returning to Warwickshire with Pascual. And yet she felt an undeniable sense of relief sweeping through her at not having to let down her clients after all.

A very special dinner had been arranged for tonight, in Pascual's honour, and a lot of hard work and organisation had gone into getting it exactly right. He might believe that her business was failing, and that she should be relieved to put it behind her, but she still felt committed to seeing it through right to the end and giving the service her clients had hired her to provide. It was a matter of pride, if nothing else.

'Of course I don't mind! You know I *love* taking care of him. Shall I come back in, say…' she glanced down at her watch '…one hour?'

'That would be great. Thanks, Mum.'

'I'll see you then.'

'She lives just down the road,' she explained as the door shut behind her.

'That must be a big help to you.'

His observation of her had not lingered over-long. Pascual had returned his attention once again to his son, who was busy delving deep into the large box to eagerly display the full extent of his impressive collection of toy cars.

'It is.'

Reaching for her mug of tea, Briana carefully sipped at the steaming hot liquid and wondered how long this apparent peace between them would last before Pascual once again demonstrated his disappointment and disapproval of her. But then, quickly becoming engaged by the only ever before imagined scene of father and son together, she determinedly put her fears aside and willed herself at least to try and relax for the moment.

* * *

He fixed his tie—then pulled the knot apart and fixed it all over again. He seemed to be all fingers and thumbs this evening, and it was not like him. *But then how was he supposed to function normally when he had just spent the afternoon with his son for the very first time?* The boy was incredible—beautiful—his own flesh and blood.

He had changed everything for Pascual. His life would no longer be the same now that he knew Adán existed. His emotions ranged from wanting to shout out his joy on discovering he was a father to complete strangers, to feeling devastated that he had missed four precious years of his child's life and would never get them back.

Pausing in front of the mahogany cheval dressing mirror, he saw the fevered glint of excitement mingled with regret in his eyes and realised the last thing he felt like doing tonight was attending a tedious business dinner—no matter how sublime the menu or how beautiful the house. Making conversation with three men he had barely anything in common with, apart from a love of playing polo, was hardly a big draw, he reflected soberly. And he was still not certain whether he wanted to sell his precious ponies to them after all.

But then Briana would be there—attending to their every need, no doubt, keen to impress her clients and do a good job, potentially rescue her failing business. Even though he was mad as hell with her for keeping Adán a secret from him, Pascual didn't doubt her lush curves and flawlessly beautiful features would compensate for having to talk business when he would much rather have spent the evening with his small son, trying to get to know him a little.

At some point during those two precious hours spent with her and their child Pascual had suddenly woken up to the reality of the fact that her business was what allowed Briana to pay the rent and put food on the table. Knowing that, he could not allow himself to deliberately make her turn her back on tonight's event. Even though it might be the last of its kind—seeing as he intended to take her and Adán back to Buenos Aires with him...

Leaving the others to their cigars and a third or fourth glass of wine at the table, Pascual excused himself and went in search of Briana. The last time she had appeared before them had been about an hour ago, and with the business part of their dinner over—he had finally decided to go through with the sale of the ponies after all—he was anxious to see her again. Her perfume had lingered in the air long after she had left them, and all through dinner it had subtly taunted him, reactivating that tight, coiled feeling deep in his belly.

Putting his head round the door of the large Tudor

kitchen where once again staff from the Michelin starred restaurant were busy packing away, he spied Tina sipping a cup of coffee and munching on a biscuit.

Her face lit up with genuine pleasure when she saw him, and she hurried across the stone-flagged floor to greet him. 'Hello. How did the dinner go?' she asked in a rush, her cheeks pinkening a little.

In return Pascual's smile was polite, but restrained. 'It was very good. The duck in particular was excellent. Please give my compliments to the chef.'

'Of course I will. Are you looking for Briana?'

'Yes…as a matter of fact, I am.'

'She had a bit of a headache, to tell you the truth, and went up to her room for a while. If there's anything you need…perhaps *I* can help?'

Feeling the tight, coiled sensation become even more intense at the memory of Briana in the classic black jersey dress with a slightly plunging neckline she had been wearing that evening, Pascual smiled again—with just a hint of wry humour. 'Thank you, but no. It is Miss Douglas I need to speak with. Goodnight, Tina.'

'Goodnight, Mr Dominguez.'

At the knock on the door, Briana sprang guiltily up from the bed, thinking immediately that it must be Tina. She had not intended to leave the younger woman on her own to cope for long, but she had needed a few moments to lie down and try and get rid of the tension headache that had plagued her ever since she and Pascual had arrived back at the house from their trip to London.

She didn't doubt it had manifested itself because of the stresses and strains of the day. The whole time Pascual had been with her and Adán she had veered between worrying about their future and being flooded with joy that at last her son and his father were together...*whatever the consequences*.

Her heart knocked wildly against her ribs when she found the man she'd been thinking about on the other side of the door, still dressed in his immaculate tuxedo, looking as if he could give James Bond himself a run for his money and then some.

'Is anything the matter?' she asked, catching her breath as his dark brooding gaze dropped to her cleavage and for a disturbing moment lingered there.

'Your colleague told me you had a headache. Can I come in?'

A wise woman would probably have told him no. But right then Briana did not feel equipped to be particularly wise *or* strong where Pascual was concerned. Not when he stood there looking like the living embodiment of her most heartfelt fantasy and greatest desire...

'I'm not up to talking very much,' she answered, lightly touching her forehead.

'That is fine with me,' he came back, the look on

his strong-boned face inscrutable. 'I do not particularly want to talk either.' The panelled door shut firmly behind him.

'Then why are you—?'

The rest of her question was cut off by the feeling of the most intensely melting pressure from Pascual's commandingly erotic mouth on hers. Then his tongue thrust deep, and Briana groaned her pleasure hungrily and out loud. His hands were firmly at the side of her ribs. His touch seemed to have the shocking capacity to burn right through the jersey material of her dress and sear the skin underneath. She *ached* for them to be everywhere at once, such was the torrent of desire that engulfed her.

Her whole body was held hostage to the heartfelt sensation of sensual aliveness that Pascual's bold passionate caresses elicited, and Briana realised she wanted even *more*. It was true she didn't feel like talking—the day's events had emotionally drained her to the marrow—but she felt even less like thinking, or offering up excuses for her recklessly wild behaviour now. In truth, thinking straight around this man had always been difficult.

Before she even knew what she was doing, she was running her fingers through the silky strands of his gleaming dark hair and arching her back, so that he could slide his hungry seeking hands into the low neckline of her dress to cup and stroke her breasts, to pinch her tight-puckered nipples inside her bra until she whimpered.

Bending his head, once again he suckled and then nipped the sensitive skin at the side of her neck with his teeth. Erotic heat sizzled through Briana's insides like a flaming thunderbolt. Temporarily losing her balance as she sagged with pleasure against his taut hard frame, she was hardly surprised when he tipped her up into his arms and carried her across the carpeted room to the bed without so much as speaking a word. She heard him relinquish his shoes and leave them by the side of the bed. Then, before she could quite get her bearings, he caught handfuls of her soft jersey dress and tugged the whole garment up over her head. Discarding it, he shrugged off his immaculate tuxedo, then his tie, closely followed by his perfectly tailored Savile Row shirt.

As Briana gazed at his tanned broad chest, with its awesome display of toned musculature and the finest dark hair swirling round his flat male nipples, she almost wanted to cry at the epitome of staggering masculine beauty that was before her.

For a moment Pascual tipped up her chin and gazed deep into her eyes. She had no clue what he was thinking. Then, once more in the grip of urgent passionate heat, and just before he attended to the zip fastener on his trousers, he hauled Briana hard against that heavenly chest of his and claimed her lips in the longest, deepest, most devastating kiss she had ever known. As his addictively spellbinding taste poured over her, like the most drugging and sensual wine she could ever imagine tasting, Briana knew right then that she had no intention of calling a halt to what was about to happen.

She caught her breath as he slid his hands round her back and unhooked her bra. On his lips was the most lascivious heart-pounding smile Briana had ever seen, and he filled his hands with the full, soft weight of her aching breasts at last. Her relief and pleasure were indescribable.

'Do you want me, Briana?' His voice was low and resonant, with a husky catch in it. 'Do you want me as much as I want *you*? It has been a long, long time…no?'

Moving his hands down to the sultry curve of her hips, Pascual removed the remainder of her clothing and then, placing his warm palm in the centre of her chest, pushed her gently back onto the plump silk pillows behind her.

Immediately she was on her back, and his mouth claimed her tight, engorged nipples in turn, suckling and laving them, his hot tongue stroking over her aching flesh like the only balm that could ever bring true ease. Sliding a hand down over her ribcage onto her flat stomach, he dipped even lower into the triangle of silky hair between her thighs. Urging them apart, he slid one finger into Briana's moist heat, then two. Such was the intensity of pressure and pleasure this act bestowed that she wondered for one starry moment how she hadn't shot right through the ceiling. Hungrily, as he moved inside her, she reached out to curve her hand round his hard velvet shaft. Memory flooded her, of the many nights just like this one when she had shared his bed and been driven half out of her mind with the joy and ecstasy his magnificent body passionately delivered to hers.

Pascual moved her hand and replaced his fingers with that most intimate part of himself, and as he thrust upwards and deep inside her Briana cried out, gripped his lean masculine hips with her thighs, wrapping the rest of her long slender legs possessively round his back.

'Kiss me!' he entreated, his dark gaze burning down into hers.

Eagerly complying, Briana hardly knew who devoured who as their lips met and melded into one. All she knew was that the sensations and feelings the contact wrought was *wonderful* and she didn't want it to stop. Just as Pascual's thrusts became more demanding and focused she felt herself start to unravel helplessly. It had been just as he had said…a long, *long* time…and her emotions were so heightened round him that she couldn't hold back either her desire or her need. Stunned, she fluttered her eyelids closed as each pulsing wave of pleasure seemed to intensify even more than the last.

Just as she was returning to earth he held himself rigid above her. His disturbing glance was as serious as Briana had ever seen it.

'Maybe now we make another baby…*sí*?'

CHAPTER SEVEN

BRIANA'S hands tightened in shock round his smooth hard biceps. 'You can't be serious?' Right up until that moment she had barely given birth control a thought, she was ashamed to admit. The realisation made her aware of just *how* reckless she could be around this man—how swept away by forces she definitely wasn't in control of. 'No! You *can't*. We *mustn't*!'

But he was moving inside her again, and the sensation of his hard, strong body joined to hers was hurtling every thought that arose crashing against rocks.

'I should have been there at my son's birth! I should have been there for him for the last four years!' Suddenly growing still, Pascual withdrew from her just before it was too late. He sat back on his heels, breathing hard.

Startled and hurt by what he had exclaimed, Briana lay there, her breath laboured, watching him as he suddenly moved further down the bed—as if he wanted to put as much distance as possible between them.

Dropping his head into his hands, he murmured some words in Spanish she didn't comprehend.

'Pascual? Pascual, are you all right?'

Pulling the silk counterpane up to her chest, she moved towards him to lay her hand on the strong broad bank of his shoulder. He flinched as though struck.

'No…I am *not* all right! It was crazy of me to come here to you. Next time I will try and show a little more restraint!'

Grabbing up his silk boxers from the end of the bed, he quickly pulled them on and then did the same with his trousers. Sliding his bare feet into his shoes, he reached for the rest of his clothing and then turned solemn-faced to survey her. His expression told her that he was in a dark haunted place where she could not reach him and it made Briana shudder.

'I feel nothing for you…*nothing*!' he declared savagely. 'Do you know that? Your body may still arouse me, but in every other respect you leave me cold. You kept me from my own son and that I can never forgive. Tomorrow I will make arrangements for our return to Buenos Aires, and from then on Adán will have the life he was meant to. As for you…you will just have to learn to make the best of what you find when you get there. It is really no concern of mine whether you will be happy or not when we marry. I will provide every material comfort you could want…but as for companionship and friendship?' His lips thinned disparagingly, 'Maybe that is something you will just have to learn to live without…just as I have had to live without it these past five years. I will see you in the morning.'

As he left, strangely *not* slamming the door as she'd expected, but closing it as if the temper that had arisen like an electrical storm on a sunny day had suddenly dissipated as abruptly as it had appeared, Briana sank back down on the bed, feeling stunned and cold. Drawing the rich purple counterpane round her now shivering shoulders, she heard Pascual's heated words echo round and round inside her head once again, bringing home to her just how deeply and irrevocably she had hurt him by keeping Adán from him.

Up until now she had resisted the whole idea of returning to Buenos Aires and the three of them making a life together there. But even though he had warned her she would have to forgo companionship and friendship as far as he was concerned, Briana wondered if she didn't *owe* it to him to give the un-conventional arrangement he was demanding a try? There might be genuine fears about not fitting into his world, just as before, but it was her fears which had driven her from Pascual in the first place and brought about the situation with Adán. *What had she got to lose?* she thought unhappily. Unless she could clear her debt her business was probably going to fold anyway—and what prospects would she have staying in the UK as a single mother, trying to raise her son all on her own and relying far too much on her own mother for help?

If Adán had his father in his life and grew up feeling safe, secure and well-loved by *both* parents, what did it signify if Briana had to sacrifice her own longing for love and companionship on the way? *She had already spent too many years alone and she should be used to it by now.* But tonight—tonight when Pascual had held her once again and for a while responded with all the passionate intensity of the most ardent lover—had rekindled that need inside her to be loved and desired and cared for by this man—a man she would willingly go to the ends of the earth for because she still felt the same way about him.

Hardly even realising that tears were spilling down her cheeks, she sighed as though her heart would crack, and felt like dying as she recalled Pascual's recent scathing words. *You leave me cold!* he had declared. That harsh announcement had made Briana feel as if she was being sliced in two.

Hardly able to bear thinking about it, she pushed aside the warm counterpane and got determinedly to her feet. Her heart might indeed be breaking, but she still had a job to do and she would do it to the very best of her ability—even if it were for the last time. As for Pascual—she had already made up her mind to tell him in the morning that she would agree to return to Buenos Aires with him. As long as his demands were reasonable and he took her views into consideration then she would not be putting any obstacles in his way.

He did not sleep well. But then he had hardly expected to after that unfortunate scene in Briana's bedroom. Sexual frustration made for a most uncomfortable bedfellow, Pascual discovered anew. And after leaving his lover's warm bed much earlier than he'd anticipated, because his anger and hurt had finally got the better of him, it was his legacy. But the truth was that for a few moments there, when the possibility had arisen for him to become a father for the second time, he had had a heartrending vision of a baby being put into his arms—something that Briana had cruelly denied him with Adán. He had longed for such a scene to become a reality.

Five years ago she had *willingly* agreed to become his bride. Now she might not be as willing, but Pascual vowed to harden his heart against that. This marriage of convenience he was determined to go ahead with might not be the romantic idyll he had foolishly once envisaged their partnership would be, but it would ensure that she would not be free to fall in love with someone else—share her body with someone else and desert him and their son.

It had been the most incredible experience to see Adán for the first time. One glance at the boy and Pascual had known straight away, with the most profound inner certainty, that he would gladly lay down his life to protect him and keep him safe. Fidel had been right about how having a child became the most important concern of a man's life—driving away all other ambition that had previously seemed so significant. *That was why he would take Briana to Buenos Aires and marry her...even if the love between them was gone for ever.*

Rubbing his chest to try and relieve some of the emotion that for a moment made it hard to breathe, he went to the window, drew back the sumptuous lined drapes and gazed out on yet another cold and frosty morning. Contemplating the scene without the pleasure he had experienced during his early-morning walk yesterday, he felt his longing to be back home in warmer climes was suddenly close to overwhelming.

On their way back to London the following morning, Briana glanced at her so far silent passenger and tightened her hands apprehensively on the steering wheel. Since bidding farewell to her clients as they got into the waiting Rolls-Royce that would take them home to their various destinations, Pascual had only spoken to her when he had absolutely *had* to. Such as when he had informed her that he was going back with her to 'sort things out', and then on to the hotel he was staying at for the duration of his stay in Park Lane.

Despondent that he was still mad at her, Briana wondered how they would sort *anything* out if he continued to be furious with her and maintain a sullen silence.

As they joined the stream of motorway traffic heading for London, a long-suffering sigh escaped her and Pascual's head immediately snapped round.

'What is wrong?' he demanded.

Ruefully shrugging her shoulders, she stole a brief glance sideways at him. 'Do you want a list?'

'If you expect me to apologise for what happened last night, then—'

'I don't,' she cut in, grimacing, 'I hurt you by not telling you about Adán, and whether you believe me or not I'm truly sorry. I also want you to know that when we get home I'll be telling him who you *really* are...that you're his father and not...not my friend.'

'Good. I see no reason in denying him the truth any longer.'

'And as for going back to Buenos Aires...' She

sensed his brooding gaze suddenly cleave even more
intensely to her profile—as she kept her eyes firmly
on the road ahead. 'I'll agree to go back with you for
a while at least, to give us time to come to some arrangement about the future. But I can't stay away too
long because I've had a court summons regarding my
business debt and I'll be in serious trouble if I'm not
there to answer it.'

'That is nothing to worry about.'

'To *you* it might not be, but it certainly *is* something to worry about as far as I'm concerned!'

'I mean that *I* will pay the debt on your behalf.
Since I am to be your husband, then naturally I will
take responsibility for it.'

'Now, wait a minute I—'

'Watch the road!'

In the blink of an eye Briana suddenly found that
they were far too close to the rear bumper of the car
in front of her. Guiltily, her stomach turning over in
fright, she eased down on her speed. 'Sorry.'

'As I said…' Pascual continued, without so much
as a hint of warmth or conciliation in his accented
voice. 'I will pay this debt for you and then you can
forget about your business.'

'Do you think what I do is so unimportant I can just
cast it aside as if it was nothing? Besides…I can hardly
forget about it when I have an employee to think of.
What will Tina do if she doesn't work for me?'

'This was the only job you've had on your books for some time, so I gather?'

'What are you saying? How did you—?' Her shoulders hunching in resignation, Briana sighed. '*Tina*. I should have guessed.'

'She has already told me that she temps from time to time in between jobs. She seems a resourceful girl to me…she will be okay. And you will have other important occupations to think of when we go back to Argentina.'

'All right… That aside…if you pay this debt for me—and I will only agree to let you do so because of Adán—then you know I will have to insist on paying you back, Pascual?'

'Now you are being foolish.'

'I won't accept your help unless you agree to let me pay you back. I mean it!'

Sighing, as if she was taxing him to the very limits of his patience, the man beside her reluctantly nodded. 'Okay, okay! Just concentrate on the road, will you? Or we will find ourselves in the hospital instead of at your house!'

'My driving's not *that* bad!'

To Briana's complete disconcertion he chuckled, and her skin broke out into tingling gooseflesh at the sound. 'Not as bad as *some* I know, I will agree.'

'I suppose you're referring to women in particular?'

Unable to prevent the sharp slash of jealousy that ripped through her at the thought of Pascual with another beautiful model like Claudia, or worse Claudia herself, her mood grew even more despondent.

'Are you jealous, *carina*?' he drawled softly.

'Let's change the subject, shall we?'

'So…today we will put your business affairs in order, and tomorrow I will organise our travel arrangements. I will also ring home and instruct Sofia to make ready a room near us for Adán.'

'Sofia is still with you?'

The older Spanish woman who was Pascual's housekeeper had always been so sweet to Briana, and she had never forgotten her kindness. Of all the people she had met when she'd stayed in Palermo, she was the one who had truly accepted her for herself and had never given her the slightest inkling that she disparaged where she came from. She'd been totally happy with Briana because Pascual—whom she revered—loved her.

'Of course!'

For a moment Pascual sounded nonplussed, as if he could hardly fathom why anyone he employed would even *think* of leaving him to work for someone else. And of course he was right. As far as Briana had been able to observe he was a fair and generous employer, and Sofia clearly *idolised* him.

'And *you*, of course,' he continued, his magnetic

voice lowering, 'will not need a room of your own—because you will be sharing *my* quarters.'

The possessive intent with which he shared this last piece of information made her hair bristle, but she held onto her indignation...*just*.

'Perhaps in the light of what happened yesterday, it might be best if we kept our relationship purely platonic?' she ventured.

'I was mad at you yesterday...but my anger at you will not interfere with the physical side of our relationship in future, I promise you.'

'Well, I—'

'There is one thing I assure you our marriage will *not* be, Briana, and that is platonic!'

'Even though I leave you cold?' The small nugget of hurt inside her chest was like a sharp stone as she remembered the insult. She sensed his glance intensify again.

'I did not say your body left me cold...far from it!'

'But—'

'Call me arrogant, if you will...but I *know* that my body does not leave *you* cold either. If nothing else we can at least take consolation in our mutual desire for each other and in being good parents.'

Biting her lip on a despondent retort, Briana concentrated all her attention on the road ahead for the rest of the trip. The only time she allowed her thoughts to wander was when she tried to imagine how Adán was going to receive the news that the man she had introduced to him yesterday as a friend was really his father…

'Do you really think this is the right thing to do, Briana?'

Standing in her daughter's kitchen, Frances Douglas cupped her hands round her recently made mug of coffee and frowned in concern.

'I honestly don't know. We'll just have to wait and see how things pan out, won't we? I feel so *torn*, Mum. It was very wrong of me to keep Adán from Pascual…I know that now. And I owe it to him to at least give this marriage he's suggesting a try. Can you imagine how he's feeling right now, learning that he's been a father for the past four years and didn't even know it?'

Pushing her hair away from her eyes, Briana leant back against the kitchen worktop and folded her arms.

'He's in the living room with Adán, down on the floor playing cars, and already they look like they're crazy about each other! Adán was so pleased to learn Pascual was his dad… His little face lit up as if he could hardly believe it. I didn't expect that. You know how reticent he can be about meeting new people, don't you? It's as though the natural bond between them was just waiting for the chance to be forged. Okay, so there's the not so small matter of Pascual living in Argentina, but it's only natural that he wants his son to be with him there. Adán can have a good life there, and we won't have to struggle any more. There are lots of pluses.'

'Adán can have a good life, you said? What about *you*, Briana?' her mother asked thoughtfully. 'Can you live with a man you've already told me can't possibly love you, who bears resentment towards you because you kept his son from him?'

'Pascual's not like Dad, Mum. I don't mean to upset you, but he wouldn't be deliberately cruel to me…I know that.'

Frances's light grey eyes—so like her daughter's—narrowed. 'Withholding love from someone has got to be about the *cruellest* thing there is in my book,' she said softly, and Briana shivered as though someone had just walked over her grave…

Buenos Aires…three days later

The heat was like a sultry tropical kiss as soon as they stepped out of the plane. Even though they were only in the airport terminal, the sense that they were somewhere much more exotic and different from home was palpable immediately. Breathing in the myriad scents and the atmosphere of being back in the city that she had embraced with such excitement and hope when she'd first arrived there five years ago, for a beguiling moment Briana felt her fears and doubts replaced by unexpected optimism.

A short time later, in the chauffeur-driven Mercedes that had been waiting to pick them up, she had a chance to view their location more closely through discreetly tinted windows, her hands in her lap and her gaze soaking up everything she saw just like a child…just as if she were seeing it all for the very first time. Someone had described the city as the 'Paris of South America', and with its sweeping boulevards and grand architecture, she could easily understand why. But Briana also knew that every *barrio* or district had its own distinct features that reflected the multiplicity of cultures that resided there. Some were not grand at all, but intimate, lively and colourful.

Next to her, Adán had fallen asleep, his curly dark head against Pascual's suited shoulder, the child's sweeping long lashes and hair the same intense sable of his father's. Glancing at them both, she felt her breath catch. That bond they seemed to have instantly forged on sight was growing ever stronger, she intuited, and would continue to deepen the more time they spent together.

'How are you feeling?' His disturbing gaze touching hers, Pascual raised an enquiring brow.

'Fine. Hardly tired at all after the journey.'

Having imagined that the trip to Argentina would raise all kinds of challenges and concerns—not least

because of the tension between herself and Pascual—
Briana had figured without the effortless reassurance
of first-class luxury travel. Her husband-to-be had
only to click his fingers, it seemed, and the attentive
flight staff would bring them anything they desired…
from a four-course gourmet meal to champagne on
ice.

Taking Pascual at his word when he had urged her
to 'rest and relax' while he chatted to their son, to her
complete surprise Briana had soon found herself
dozing comfortably in her luxurious seat in the blissfully quiet first-class cabin, and in no time at all it
seemed they had arrived in Argentina.

'I meant how do you feel about being back in
Buenos Aires?'

*Nervous, apprehensive, scared you'll keep on
punishing me and I won't be able to stand it…*
Clutching her slender hands tighter in her lap, Briana
bravely met Pascual's penetrating unsmiling glance,
then sighed. 'I can't tell you that yet. It's a bit like a
dream right now.'

'Not a nightmare?'

For a startling moment Briana saw a flash of what
she thought was genuine apprehension on Pascual's
arresting face, but he seemed to recover quickly and
revert to complete control of his emotions—as
though that possible moment of doubt and fear had
never transpired.

'Not a nightmare…no. I—'

'I have been in touch with Marisa and Diego…remember them?' he cut in, his tone lighter.

'Of course I remember them!' A burst of warmth infiltrated Briana's tense insides as she recalled the affluent couple she had worked for once upon a time— the couple in whose house she had first met Pascual.

'Sabrina…their little girl…she must be—what? Nearly six now?'

'That's right. They are looking forward to seeing you again—and to meeting Adán of course.'

'You told them—you told them about Adán?'

She saw his jaw briefly harden. 'Did you think I would *not* tell my closest friends about the fact that I have a son?'

Putting her hands briefly up to her face, Briana shook her head. 'I didn't mean it like that. I was…I suppose I'm just a bit nervous about meeting people who knew me before. People who knew me when I was with you.'

'Because you fear their judgement? Marisa and Diego have too much innate good sense and class to be influenced by what others say.'

This announcement hardly reassured Briana. She was too busy wondering what kind of reception she would receive from Pascual's family when she finally met them again, and fearing the encounter would merely confirm their worst thoughts about her. That she had proved to them she wasn't worthy of marrying Pascual five years ago, and she was even *less* worthy now!

CHAPTER EIGHT

HEADING north, they soon arrived in Palermo, where Pascual's impossibly grand and palatial house was situated. Remembering the first time she had seen it, having already been bowled over by the size and beauty of Marisa and Diego's spectacular residence, just a few lanes away, Briana could still recall her jaw dropping at her first glimpse of the dazzling white mansion with its secluded drive lined with acacia and tipuana trees.

It looked no less beautiful and imposing now, resplendent in the late-afternoon sunshine, and not for the first time she was seized with nerves at seriously contemplating living there for good. The parallels with her experience of living two weekends out of four with her father in his large house in Dorset—far less grand than this—still hovered painfully in her mind. She hadn't *ever* fitted in there, nor been made welcome, and she wondered how she would fare now in Pascual's palatial home. Trepidation was gathering inside her at the prospect of seeing his family again…especially his mother Paloma, who had disliked Briana on sight.

Drawing her attention firmly back to the present, Adán stirred, suddenly wide awake and alert. His big eyes wide, he sat up and stared curiously through the tinted windows of the car at the huge mansion looming up in front of them. He had never travelled on a plane before, nor been abroad, so this was a day of firsts he would probably always remember.

Affectionately, Briana gave his small shoulders a squeeze. 'We're here, darling.' She smiled.

'You mean this is Daddy's house?' he asked, dark eyes round as saucers.

'*Sí, hijo.* . This is my house—and yours too.' The small boy between them was not the only one who had excitement and pride reflected in his gaze. In fact, if Briana wasn't mistaken, there was a definite glint of moisture in Pascual's eyes as well. This was a momentous occasion for him, she realized—and not just because his son had just referred to him as 'Daddy' for the first time. He was a proud man—proud of his family, his country and his lineage. To bring his son home at last meant *everything* to him.

'And what about Mummy?' Adán demanded, a momentary frown on his clear smooth brow. 'Is it her house too?'

Her heart racing, she found herself under Pascual's disturbing intense scrutiny once again. Briana swore she could hear the sound of her own blood rushing through her veins.

'*Sí*, Adán… This will be your mother's home as well from now on. We will all live here together.'

Their glances met and held, and a frisson of electricity buzzed through her whole system, radiating from deep inside her womb and making her more intimately aware of him than was frankly comfortable or desirable, given the circumstances.

How did she do that? Pascual wondered, feeling dazed. Look at him with such a relatively innocent glance and make him immediately long to be alone with her, so that he could tear off her clothing with barely restrained urgency and join his aching needy body to hers…so that he could breathe her breath and taste her beguiling flavours until he was intoxicated—drunk on sensuality and desire so that he barely knew his own name any more. No woman before or since had ever made him feel like that. How he had walked out on her the other night he did not know. Except that fury and pain had overcome him and he had not been able to contain it. That would not happen the next time he found himself in bed with her! he vowed.

As the car drew up in front of the wide gleaming

steps that led to the double-doored entrance, Pascual forced himself to attend to the present as his chauffeur smartly came round to open the car doors. Taking Adán with him as he left the vehicle, he scooped the little boy up high into his arms against his chest. Waiting a moment or two for Briana to join them, and admiring the tantalising glimpse of slender thigh as her blue silk skirt revealingly rode up as she left the passenger seat, he even managed a smile in her direction before leading the way into the house.

And if at that moment he felt proud, possessive and protective of his newly acquired family—then let no man *dare* to question or blame him! Right then he did not even want to question his *own* need to include Briana as family.

'Señor Dominguez!'

Sofia—brimming with happiness and comfortingly familiar in gleaming white blouse and black-tiered skirt—greeted him as he stepped inside onto the black and white marble floor, Adán in his arms and Briana hanging back a little as though shy. Totally spontaneously he reached for her hand and pulled her to his side, pleasure exploding inside him like a firecracker at the impossibly soft touch of her skin.

'*Holà*, Sofia!' Grinning at the barely contained joy that radiated from the older woman's face, noting her eager glance dart from Adán to himself and then Briana, as if all her Christmases and birthdays had come at once, he wasn't surprised when she got out a lacy white handkerchief and dabbed at her eyes.

'I am so, *so* happy to see you all back safe!' she declared, in clear, well-spoken English. 'And to see the little one…your *son*…I can hardly believe it!' Jamming the dainty white square back into the fulsome pocket of her skirt, she slid her hands round Adán's startled face and proceeded to kiss him soundly on both cheeks. '*Holà*, Adán…I am Sofia, and I am honoured to meet you.'

'He is a little shy,' Pascual said tenderly as he set Adán on his feet and slid a reassuring arm round his shoulders. Glancing round at Briana, he gripped her hand more tightly for a moment, surprised to feel her tremble. 'And you remember Briana, Sofia?'

'*Sí*…of *course* I remember her!'

Without preamble, the housekeeper pulled Briana towards her for an enthusiastic hug, and after observing the younger woman's initial stiffness in the other woman's arms Pascual sensed his own breath ease out when he saw her slender shoulders drop a little. She hugged Sofia back.

'It's lovely to see you again, Sofia. Are you well?' she asked, stepping back to Pascual's side, her previously apprehensive expression transformed by a smile.

'*Sí, señorita*…I am *very* well…*estupendo* now that you are all here!'

'Sofia?' Addressing his housekeeper and speaking

in their native Spanish, Pascual told her they would
all like to go to their rooms and freshen up a little
before dinner. He was sure that Adán *especially*
would like to see the room that would be his. He also
asked her to instruct his chauffeur to bring in their
luggage and ask Carlo—his groundsman and
gardener—if he would kindly transport it upstairs.
That done, Pascual turned to Briana, one hand still
firmly holding onto his son's. 'I have told Sofia that
we would like to go up to our rooms. Shall we?'

Having inspected his own very large bedroom—
Briana was sure the ground floor of her whole *house*
would have fitted into the square footage it commanded!—Adán was now busy running from the huge
en-suite marble bathroom in his father and Briana's
room back into the bedroom, and then through the
opened patio doors onto the generous-sized balcony,
examining everything just as though he had been let
loose in Hamleys toy store in Regent Street.

'Slow down!' she called out to him as he exited
the balcony and ran back again into the bathroom.
'You'll wear yourself out!'

'He is happy…no?'

Suddenly Pascual was in front of her, his dark
gaze travelling at leisure down the front of her scoop-
necked white T-shirt and pastel skirt. An unexpectedly warm smile touched his lips as Briana tried

desperately *not* to look at the huge canopied empress bed to the side of her. Heat prickled all the way down her spine as she studied him.

'You promised him an adventure and he's certainly got it! He'll sleep like a top tonight after all the excitement.'

Self-consciously she folded her arms across her chest. Reaching out, Pascual tugged them free. His hand inadvertently glanced against her breast and a shocked breath escaped her.

Gravel-voiced, he said, 'Stop hiding yourself...I want to look at you.'

'I'm not hiding! You—you make me nervous sometimes. That's all.'

As if her words surprised him, he dropped his hands to his hips, and another easy smile broke free from his sensual lips.

'Well, I do not mean to make you nervous. Not today, anyway. You are a very beautiful woman, Briana, and I intend to appreciate that fact. You cannot tell me that no other man has called you beautiful since we parted?'

Where was this leading? Was he jealous? For a moment the thought made her heart leap. To be jealous of compliments paid by other men suggested he still cared...even a little. If he had feelings towards her other than just anger and blame, then that had to bode well for the future, didn't it?

'I haven't been interested in other men since—'

'Since you left me?'

The dark eyes that resembled the most stunning jet in the world briefly reflected their disappointment and pain, and Briana came crashing back down to earth again.

'I hope that's true…that you haven't seen any other men since me,' Pascual continued somberly. 'I do not like to think of you with someone else… someone who has spent time with you and my son when I could not.'

'Well, you don't have to worry. I told you…I've been too busy raising Adán and trying to run a business to have time to even *think* about dating!'

Just as she was about to quiz him on whether *he* had dated other people since they parted—yet perversely not really wanting to hear about that at all— their son diverted her.

'Mummy, can I see the garden?' Running back into the bedroom from the balcony, Adán glanced hopefully from Briana to his father.

'Yes, of course you can see the garden! We have more than one, you know? In fact we call it a park, and it has many things to see in it—like fountains, marble statues, and a very large lake!' Catching hold of the little boy's hand with a grin that was more than a match for the dazzling Argentinian sunshine, Pascual looked as pleased and happy as his son at the prospect of showing him round his home. The sight of them together squeezed Briana's heart. 'Come with me and I will give you the guided tour. Then you can come back and tell Mummy what you think.'

'Can I, Mummy?'

'Yes, that's fine. Just stay with Daddy and don't go getting yourself lost!' She faltered on the word 'Daddy' just the tiniest bit, but told herself she would soon get used to using it. One astonishing fact was becoming more and more obvious…Adán was having no trouble using it at all!

'He will never leave my sight…I promise.'

Once again Pascual confounded Briana with a smile that was laden with warmth, and once again she sensed all her defences dissolve beneath its devastating impact.

'Why don't you take a shower or a bath while you have the chance? It might help you relax after all the travelling. Carlo will leave our luggage by the door.'

'Thanks…maybe I'll do that.'

'*Bien*! We will see you later!'

He had instructed Sofia to make ready the smaller, more intimate dining room in the house, rather than the grand one used for entertaining. And now, as they sat round the large ebony table that had been beautifully and lovingly laid with the best silver cutlery and colourful patterned native crockery, Pascual surveyed his small family with pride and a growing possessiveness he could not deny. His chef had prepared the most appetising meal in honour of his son and wife-to-be, and they were lingering at the table long after they'd finished dessert. He poured Briana another glass of Malbec—a popular wine often drunk in the region—his avid glance surveying her for probably the hundredth time, in a demure white gypsy dress that showed off her pretty shoulders to perfection.

'I wanted to discuss something,' she said, fingering the delicate stem of her wine glass but not raising it to her lips.

'Of course.'

Feeling more relaxed than he had in ages, Pascual settled comfortably back into his chair.

'When we return here for good—' she briefly pulled her gaze from his to let it momentarily rest on their son '—we'll need to find a school for Adán. He's in kindergarten back home, but in a few months' time he'll be five. Is there anywhere nearby that might be suitable?'

'I will do some research. Sabrina de La Cruz—Diego and Marisa's daughter—goes to a small private school not far away, and she is extremely happy there so they tell me. I will ask them for some more information.'

'Thank you. I'd appreciate that.'

'Of course I will not just take their word for it. In the next few days we will arrange a visit there and go and see the place for ourselves. I will also find out if there is a kindergarten at the school for Adán. It might be nice for him to continue going if he has become used to it, and he will make some new friends too. Being with the other children will also help him to learn Spanish.'

'Will there be any English-speaking teachers?'

'Of course. Argentina is home to many different cultures, as you know, and we have many English-speaking inhabitants...including teachers.'

Noisily laying down his dessert spoon beside the second bowl of chocolate ice cream he'd eagerly asked for but clearly could not finish, Adán yawned and rubbed at his eyes.

'I think it's past your bedtime, my angel.' Fondly, Briana squeezed the small chubby hand on the table next to her. 'It's been a long day for you, hasn't it?' Keeping a close eye on the sleepy little boy, she turned her gaze back to Pascual. 'There is one other thing...'

He frowned. 'What is it?'

'I know you suggested I should fold my business and put it behind me now that you've paid off my debt...but what am I to do all day when Adán is at school, Pascual? I want to pay back the money I owe you. I have to have a job of some sort. I can't just sit around and be idle.'

He thought of several of his friends' wives, who didn't work at all and seemed more than content to shop, travel, and dress in the most up-to-date *haute-couture* fashion, being a decorative adjunct to their successful well-heeled husbands at dinner parties and polo matches.

Pascual had known from the first time he had met Briana that she was not a woman who would be remotely satisfied with such a way of life, and he did not blame her. He had even suggested she go to college and train for a career that appealed to her. *Until such time as their children came along, of course…* Now he took his time considering what she had said. He sensed her concern. Understood it too. They might not be contemplating the most idyllic of unions, after what had transpired between them, but the trouble was, as he gazed at her lovely face across the dinner table, Pascual kept forgetting that he wasn't in love with her any more.

A wave of heat consumed him at the thought that she would be sharing his bed tonight…and *every* other night for the foreseeable future, if he had his way.

'What if I have a word with some of my own business contacts and see if there isn't a demand for the kind of hospitality services you offer in the UK? We could set you up in business here in Buenos Aires. How would that be?'

The relief and pleasure in her expression was instantaneous. 'Really? You would do that for *me*?'

He did not know right then why he should think of what she told him about her 'schizophrenic' upbringing, her father who had called her his 'regrettable mistake', but once the thought had surfaced it was not easily relinquished. He wondered how any father could not recognise the many gifts a lovely daughter could bring and—not only that—want the best that life could offer her.

'*Sí,*' he answered thoughtfully. 'I would do that for you.'

'Señor Dominguez! Señor Dominguez! I am so sorry to interrupt, but—'

'Take a breath, Sofia!'

The small party glanced towards the dining room entrance in unison as the plump, flushed-faced housekeeper suddenly appeared in the doorway, looking as if she'd negotiated the long and winding staircase up to their landing at breakneck speed.

'What is the almighty panic?'

'Your parents and your cousin have arrived! They heard that you were back and—'

'How did they hear?' Immediately Pascual got to his feet, his dark gaze narrowing suspiciously.

'Your mother rang earlier this morning and I told her you were returning with your fiancée and your son… Did I do wrong, Señor Dominguez?'

Sighing, Pascual pushed his fingers through his thick dark hair. Frankly, this was one impromptu visit he could do without! His plan had been to phone his family the following day, after a good night's rest, and inform them of what had transpired in England—how he had met up with Briana again and learned that he had a son.

He hardly needed to be a mind-reader to know *exactly* what his suspicious mother's thoughts would have been when she'd heard the news! Top of the list would no doubt be that Briana had somehow black-mailed him into taking her back, wrongly convincing him that the child she'd borne was *his* when in actual fact he was the offspring of some other man. Well…she would only have to set eyes on Adán to know immediately who his father was!

'What shall I do, *señor*?' Looking a little distressed, Sofia waited for instructions.

'Show them into the downstairs drawing room and get them some drinks,' he answered curtly. Then, deliberately softening his tone, he said, 'Tell them we will be down in a few minutes. *Gracias*, Sofia.'

'*Sí, señor.*'

Abruptly the housekeeper turned and went back the way she'd come.

The tension in the room was as taut as the atmosphere in an aeroplane after take-off had been inexplicably delayed. Immediately Pascual met Briana's large grey eyes, and saw the worry and strain reflected there.

'It will be okay,' he said lightly, privately knowing that nothing was *ever* that simple or clear-cut when it came to his passionate-natured mother, and wishing again that he could have delayed this meeting until tomorrow at least.

'Will it?' She was rising to her feet, and with her hand on top of their son's curly dark head she sighed. 'I don't mind so much for myself if accusations are going to be leveled,' she told him, raising her chin, 'but I *do* mind that Adán might be upset in any way.'

She was as protective and fierce as any feral creature around her cub, Pascual saw, and an unexpected bolt of admiration jolted through him at the knowledge.

'You'll see she's done a good job in raising him,' Briana's mother had asserted, and already he was finding that to be perfectly true.

Considering his visitors downstairs, he reflected that it was fortunate his father was there tonight—because if anyone could get Paloma Dominguez to see sense and calm down then it was Iago. He had been far less judgemental of Briana, he recalled, regret shooting through him that he had not addressed the matter of his parents' less than warm reception of his bride-to-be before.

'I will simply introduce him to my parents and then ask Sofia to take him up to bed. I promise you I will not tolerate any upset caused to him either.'

He saw her slender shoulders relax a little before

she leaned down towards Adán, helping him out of the large dining chair that left his little legs dangling several inches from the floor.

'Thank you,' she murmured. Reaching for a starched linen napkin, she cleaned the chocolate ice cream stains from around his mouth, then kissed the top of his head. 'There, poppet…now you're fit to be seen by the Queen of England herself!'

'We had better go down, then.'

Gesturing towards the door, Pascual waited for them to precede him into the long, high-ceilinged corridor, with its six suspended crystal chandeliers, and privately vowed that if his mother caused any distress to either of them then he would not hesitate to tell her in no uncertain terms to leave his house and not come back until she could learn to be more civil…

CHAPTER NINE

As Briana and Pascual entered the room, with Adán between them, the three adults who had been waiting for them stood up in unison from the luxurious armchairs they'd been occupying. Immediately the sight filled Briana's heart with apprehension and dread. *They must despise her for what she'd done to their son.* A reunion hardly boded well under the circumstances…how could it?

But just then Pascual gently touched his hand to the back of her waist, and, intuiting that he was giving her his support, she felt a surge of deep gratitude ripple through her. Her determination not to be intimidated renewed, she lifted her chin and made her lips form a smile.

'*Holà!*' His resonant voice impinging on the tension-filled silence, Pascual walked forward to embrace his parents and cousin in turn, before returning to Briana's side.

The frighteningly elegant and slim Paloma Dominguez—with her slanted feline eyes, faultless make-up and classically beautiful *haute-couture* clothing—was a formidable sight at the best of times, and she was not one to be slow in vocalising her opinion on anything. But everyone appeared to lapse into a stunned silence as they glanced in Briana's direction, and she was acutely aware that their attention was focused on the little boy holding her hand, rubbing his eyes and yawning.

In English, and with pride in his voice, Pascual smiled and announced clearly, 'This is my son—Adán.'

It was Iago Dominguez—his father—who moved first. A little broader of girth these days, than Briana remembered, he was still an extremely imposing and attractive man for his age. Now, with no trouble at all, he dropped down easily to the same level as Adán and, his brown eyes clearly emotional, in wonderment reached out to stroke the tips of his fingers across Adán's baby-soft cheek. '*Holà*, Adán. *Soy su abuelo…* I am your grandfather… Did you know that you look just like your *papà* did when he was your age?'

Adán was shaking his head in reply and his small hand gripped Briana's a little tighter.

'Well, little one…you do. The likeness is incredible!' Standing up to his full height again, Iago now surveyed Briana with an emotional glance. 'He is a fine boy,' he declared a little gruffly. 'But you were wrong to walk out on my son and cause him such distress…also to keep from us all the fact that you had had his child! What can have possessed you to do such a thing?'

Before Briana could get past the dryness in her mouth to speak, Pascual stepped in, his hand reassuringly at her back again. 'Have you ever thought that you and rest of the family might have played your part in driving Briana away, Father?' he suggested. 'Think how hard it was for her to come and live amongst us— to leave her home, her family, her friends, and then not to feel exactly welcomed by my own family?'

'We did not know her very well back then. She was unknown to us…all but a stranger…and it takes time to get to know someone, does it not?'

'You did not act as if you wanted to get to know her at all! You kept her at a distance, and I fooled myself that it was not happening instead of telling you that your behaviour was unacceptable.'

It warmed Briana beyond measure that Pascual was standing up for her. It gave her the courage to speak out as she had never spoken out to his parents before.

'I wanted you to like me…to accept me—at least for Pascual's sake, if not my own. My own father rejected me, and when I saw that it might be the same again for me, living here in Buenos Aires amongst people who treated me in a similar manner…well, it brought back some of those unhappy feelings I'd had as a child and I was naturally apprehensive.'

Behind Iago—who was suddenly looking thoughtful—his wife Paloma moved towards them with an expression that was completely bereft of the new consideration reflected in her husband's. Her cool gaze seemed as distant as it had always been to Briana as it haughtily scanned her features.

'Why did you keep my son's child from him?' she demanded without preamble.

Even Iago looked uncomfortable at her outburst. Her heart thudding heavily inside her chest, Briana resolved to just be herself when answering the blunt question. *No more hiding behind a mask of politeness or not feeling good enough*, she vowed, or she might inadvertently cause Adán to believe *he* wasn't good enough either.

'I made a mistake,' she answered quietly, brushing her hair from the side of her face and sensing Pascual's hand behind her back, stroking her. 'No doubt I made *lots* of mistakes when Pascual and I were together. But we both should have been more open and not kept our fears and worries to ourselves. I can see that now. It was wrong of me to keep Adán from him and I honestly regret it.'

'My son is a good man. Even if you did not feel that *we* accepted you, you should have stayed with him regardless. Not run away!'

Feeling torn, Briana bit down anxiously on her lip. But then Pascual was sliding his arm completely round her waist, giving her a brief smile before addressing the woman who stood before them.

'Unfortunately Briana witnessed something between myself and Claudia the night of the party that made her believe I would not stay faithful to her in our marriage. *That* was what forced her decision to leave.'

'Something happened between you and Claudia?' Iago asked in surprise, his dark gaze probing his son's.

'It was nothing. She had had too much to drink, that's all. But to Briana it looked like I was encouraging her foolish attentions when I categorically was not!'

Her cheeks flushing a little, Paloma Dominguez added her own comment—and it was not what Briana expected at all.

'My husband is right…Adán *does* look very much like Pascual as a child.'

As if the annoyance she had previously emitted had ebbed away beneath the infiltration of a much stronger, more powerful emotion, the older woman bent down to the little boy and kissed him soundly on both cheeks. With tears in her eyes she impelled his small body into her arms and threaded long slim fingers with an array of dazzling jewelled rings affectionately through his mass of dark curls.

Amazingly, Adán did not struggle or put up a

protest. Hardly able to believe what she was seeing, Briana was all but lost for words.

'I am starting to feel left out!' Grinning, Pascual's handsome cousin Rafa suddenly appeared before her and enfolded her in a friendly hug. '*Holà*, Briana. You are even more bewitching than I remember!'

Unable to help herself, Briana wondered if he was still going out with Claudia, Pascual's ex. Her pulse raced a little at the memory of that night five years ago, when Rafa had arrived with her at the party and the evening had ended so disastrously with her seeing the beautiful blonde model kissing her husband-to-be.

'You're looking well yourself Rafa.' She smiled, and suddenly her pulse was racing again, because Pascual had drawn her even nearer to him, and the sensation of his warm, hard body next to hers made her knees feel suddenly and alarmingly weak.

'He was hoping you would say that,' he teased, but there was a distinct warning in his glance as he rested it briefly on his cousin, Briana noticed. A warning that said *Do not overstep the mark because she is mine*. It made her insides flutter.

'Mummy, I'm tired!'

Feeling a tug on the hem of her dress, she saw a wan-faced Adán, gazing hopefully up at her.

'I should take him to bed.' Turning towards the man at her side, she waited until he nodded in agreement.

Without preamble he scooped his son up into his

arms and surveyed the assembled company. 'He has had a very long day,' he told them. 'Enjoy your drinks, and Briana and I will be back shortly.'

They all kissed the bemused and by now *very* sleepy child goodnight, and before she knew it she and Pascual were climbing the impossibly grand winding staircase with its opulent tread up to the little boy's bedroom.

'You are very quiet tonight.'

Leaving the dressing room that was adjacent to the master bedroom, Pascual found Briana seated on the bed. The sleeves of her cotton knee-length pink robe were rolled up to the elbows and she was smoothing lotion onto her pale exposed forearms. With the light application of make-up she usually wore cleaned away, and her dark hair swept up behind her head with wisps of escaped tendrils framing her face and neck, he thought she had never looked more lovely…or more alluring.

As had been the case from almost the very first moment he had ever set eyes on her, desire followed swiftly and intensely on the heels of that captivating thought, like a waterfall plunging down over a cliff-face.

'I was miles away, actually.'

Shyly surveying him, her ethereal grey eyes were like twin beams of silver starlight in the softly lamp-lit room, and Pascual sensed the heat in him move fiercely through his body like a sirocco wind threatening a previously calm desert.

'What were you thinking about?' Dropping down next to her, clad only in black silk pyjama bottoms, he realized even the minimum of clothing was too hot against his skin at the mere sight of this woman. Quizzically, he smiled at her.

'I was thinking about seeing your parents and Rafa again,' she replied, continuing to rub the lotion into her skin, seemingly oblivious to the effect she was having on him. 'I am glad that we all seemed to let down our guard a little. Perhaps in future my relationship with them can be a little better than I imagined it ever could? I hope so, anyway.'

'I should have listened to you before—when we were first together. If I had spoken to my family then perhaps our own relationship would have had a proper chance…hmm?' Pascual reflected, becoming more and more fascinated by the rhythmic movements of her small hand with its lilac-painted fingernails back and forth across her arm.

Sliding his fingers beneath her chin, he made her turn to face him. Her enchanting lips in their naked beauty quivered a little. Immediately he wanted to plunder them and wet them, make them look beestung, as he remembered they had whenever they'd made love in the past…

'But you stood up for me tonight…that makes all the difference in the world.'

'I wish I had done it before…I am well aware that my mother in particular can be a little aloof sometimes, and with people who do not know her well that may easily be misinterpreted. But I want you to know that underneath that difficult exterior she only wants the best for her family. I hope that in time you will discover that for yourself, Briana. Building good relationships will take time for all of us. But you and I are back together, after a long time apart, and feelings on all sides are bound to be tender. Can we not just put any hurts aside…for tonight at least?'

'We can. At least your parents were happy to meet Adán.'

'They were completely overjoyed at the realisation that they have a beautiful grandson. How could anyone not love him on sight? He is perfect…just perfect.'

'Already he seems to be comfortable with you and your family… It's extraordinary, really. He's only had just my mum and me for so long, and now we've come all this way to Argentina and he's totally taken everything in his stride. Sleeping in a huge bedroom on his own on his first night here is a really big deal for a small boy, do you know that? If he wakes in the night and is fearful you don't mind him coming in with us, do you?'

'Of course not. I want my son to be happy, not frightened.'

'Good. The fact is, he'll probably be missing my mum too.'

He thought of Frances Douglas, and the way she had taken him aside the day he had collected Briana and Adán to drive them to the airport—the beseeching, yet steely look in her eyes when she'd ordered him to, 'Take good care of them both, won't you? They mean everything in the world to me.'

Pascual suddenly knew a surprising need to reassure the woman by his side. 'She is welcome to come and stay whenever she wants to. I will organise the flights and pay for everything. As you can see…there is plenty of room for guests here.'

'Thanks…I appreciate that. I expect she's missing Adán too, even though we've only just left. They're naturally very close.' Stifling a yawn, Briana capped the tube of lotion and laid it down on the silk coverlet beside her. Her glance was apologetic. 'Sorry. All of a sudden I feel immensely tired. Must be all the travelling today.'

'Here.' Picking up the discarded lotion, Pascual flipped opened the top again. 'Let me apply some for you.'

'I'm done, Pascual. I don't need you to—'

'It smells of peaches…a peach for a peach…' He smiled, squeezing some of the cream into his hand. 'Turn round and loosen your robe. I will massage your shoulders for you.'

'It's all right. I don't really—'

'You do not like me touching you?'

The idea made him freeze. Already he was having immense trouble keeping his hands off her heavenly body, just sitting near her. The idea that Briana might not welcome his touch after all was akin to ice water being poured down his back, and the memory of her rejection of him as her prospective husband five years ago still had the power to wound him greatly.

'I—I didn't say I didn't like you touching me. It's just that it's late, and…'

It came to him that she was suddenly somehow shy with him. He wondered if what had happened the last time they were in bed together was on her mind. With all his heart he wanted to erase the unfortunate scene from her memory and replace it with a far happier one. So, with a slow, teasing smile, utilising his free hand, he undid the belt of her robe and eased the material down over her shoulders. Conveniently, the thin satin cerise nightgown she wore underneath had narrow spaghetti straps. Silently speculating if she had worn it especially for his benefit, Pascual saw how easy it would be to do as he'd suggested.

'Turn round, Briana. This will make you feel good…I promise.'

He had the magical touch of a healer, Briana thought in delight, with a heartfelt inner sigh. And not only did those amazing hands heal as they massaged her already overheated skin, they stirred the passion slumbering inside her into a restless wild sea that engulfed her. So much so that it was almost impossible for her to sit still on that magnificent opulent bed with the heat of Pascual's semi-naked taut-muscled body behind her, goading her imagination to ever more stimulating heights.

When he eased her robe off completely, in an orchestrated sensual manoeuvre that couldn't help but elicit a startled response from her, then slipped the thin straps of her nightgown down so low over her arms that her breasts were suddenly exposed to the warm scented night air, she sucked in a shaky breath that seemed to echo round the entire room.

'*Amante*…you are so beautiful you make my very *soul* ache for wanting you!'

His hot mouth suckled her bare shoulder as his hands circled her ribcage to massage and cup her breasts, his thumbs and forefingers stroking, then squeezing the rigid nipples, until Briana cried out and tipped back her head against his chest to allow him even greater access.

This time Pascual kissed her in the sensitive hollow between her neck and shoulder, his hands moving hungrily down to her hips, moulding them seductively in his palms. Kneeling on the bed behind her, he pressed himself against her, so that she felt the hard silk contours of his amazing body, smelled the masculine scent that had always had the power to drive her crazy. She ached so hard for his possession that she thought she might lose her mind if she couldn't have what she so desperately craved...

As if reading her mind, Pascual urged her round to face him and helped her dispense with her nightgown and robe completely. Lying down on the bed, his dark head against the silk pillows, he encouraged her to straddle that taut hard middle of his. Immediately her soft inner thighs made contact with the deliciously warm skin beneath her Briana was devastatingly reminded of the unmatched intoxicating pleasure his touch could arouse. Feverishly seeking his mouth, she bent her head for his equally feverish kiss, lips, teeth and tongues clashing hungrily, until she thought the world could come to an end right then and she wouldn't even notice.

'I need to see to something.' His ebony eyes glazed with passion, Pascual reached towards one of the elegant oak cabinets beside the bed. His lips parting in the most bone-melting smile known to woman, he opened the slim foil package he'd retrieved and handed the contents to Briana. 'Put it on for me.'

The timbre of his captivating voice was like brushed velvet to her already impossibly heightened senses, and with her heart racing she sat back a little, to ease the black silk pyjamas down over bronzed hips as lean and straight as an arrow and release him.

His sex was silky, hard and impressive, and as she nervously rolled the latex protection down over its erect length her hands were trembling.

'Now, come here…' He smiled, sliding his hands onto her thighs and urging her across him.

He entered her in one smooth, shattering thrust, and Briana's ensuing moan resonated with relief, pleasure, longing and a deep sense of being home at last. Home with the man she irrevocably now knew she had never stopped loving…not even for an instant. All the years they'd spent apart had done was increase that longing and love for him. Helplessly she thought back to when she'd given birth to Adán, and how her heart had cracked loud enough for the whole of London to hear because Pascual had not been with her to share her joy.

'That feels so good…'

Reaching for her hand, he kissed the inside of her palm as she moved over him, her hips rhythmically meeting his, feeling his possession become deeper and deeper, until she thought the deliciously wild feelings building inside her could only implode and take her straight into another stratosphere altogether.

'*How* good?' she teased, gripping and then releasing her feminine muscles tightly round him, eliciting a melting groan from deep inside his chest.

'Do you want to make me lose my mind, *amante*?' he answered, gravel-voiced, sliding his hands up her ribcage to her breasts and palming them.

Meeting his hungry, melting gaze that was like all the midnight-black skies she had ever known melded into one, Briana touched her aching mouth to his and kissed him. Voraciously his tongue slid between her lips and took command of the erotic little dance she had started, his hands sliding up and down her slim back and round to her bottom.

After a while she raised her head and now, on the most intimate terms with those black-coffee-dark eyes with their sweeping long lashes, she smiled. 'Why don't we lose our minds together?'

'Why not?' he agreed, and thrust high into her core, holding himself there as he sensed her unravel around him, showing no mercy as her shuddering soft cries littered the air.

The action was the catalyst for Pascual's own undoing. Just as he felt Briana come apart, the intense need and hunger for release that had gripped him almost from the moment she'd obligingly and so erotically sheathed him with the protection he'd given her peaked, taking him hotly and irrevocably over the edge. Now it was his turn to cry out, and as he did so he impelled Briana towards him, hungrily drowning out his own voice with the pressure of her sweet strawberry and vanilla mouth gliding against him. Then, pushing his fingers though her soft dark hair, he kept her there for long, heart-pounding seconds...

CHAPTER TEN

SHE woke to the fragrant twin scents of jasmine and jacaranda, drifting up through the opened French doors that led onto the ornate bedroom balcony. She remembered that although it was now autumn in London, it was spring in Buenos Aires. Breathing out a sigh of deep contentment—instigated, she was sure, by the pleasant 'well-loved' feeling in her body this morning—Briana was a little taken aback to find Pascual already gone from their bed.

Just as she was reaching for her cotton robe, which lay across the silk counterpane, the door opened and Adán—still dressed in his short-sleeved pyjamas—raced across the room and flung himself beside her.

'Mummy! I slept *all* night in my new bed!' he announced happily, winding his soft childish arms round her waist.

Briefly nuzzling the warmth of his sweet-smelling neck, Briana hugged him hard and gave him a kiss.

'I know you did, my darling…well done! You're getting more and more grown up every day!'

'But not *too* grown-up, hmm?' remarked the man who'd entered the room behind him. Fully dressed in light blue denim jeans and a fitted black T-shirt that instantly drew her appreciative glance to his bronzed skin and tight toned biceps, Pascual gave her a smile. 'Childhood is a precious time…we do not want him growing up too fast!'

Before she could raise a comment he reached the side of the bed and, bending down, pressed his warm lips to her cheek. Instantly the provocative drift of his spicy cologne and his own unique male scent made a devastating assault on Briana's senses, and the passion of the night they had shared came back to her in all its never-to-be forgotten glory. *She blushed.*

'Buenos diás,' he added, dark eyes twinkling.

His comment about Adán not growing up too fast was all the more poignant, she reflected, because he had already missed over four years of his son's life. Her eyes briefly smarted as she fought to hold back her tears.

'Good morning. You should have woken me. Adán needs a shower—and so do I.'

'Take your time. I will see to Adán and you can shower and dress at your leisure. Then we will meet downstairs for breakfast. How does that sound?'

'Good…if you don't mind seeing to him? His clothes are folded away in the bureau in his bedroom.'

'Come on, *mi hijo*! Let us leave your *mamà* in peace for a little while, to do all the things that beautiful ladies have to do in the morning to get ready for the day…*sí*?'

Catching Briana's eye, Pascual gave her the most lascivious wink, and her skin suddenly felt like ice cream melting beneath the blaze of a scorching sun. To disguise her disturbing reaction and divert herself, she gave Adán a brief, affectionate squeeze, and helped him off the edge of the bed onto the floor.

'Go with—go with Daddy, sweetheart, and I will see you soon.'

'Can I play in the park again today?' She heard his sweet voice beseeching Pascual as they went towards the door, hand in hand. 'I want to see the fountain and the lake again!'

'Of course. But first we must have breakfast with your mother…*sí*?'

Jogging across the lush grass, with his small son just ahead of him, Pascual thought that he was possibly the most content that he had been for a long, long time. *God had sent him a miracle, in the shape of the sweet child before him, and the woman he had once adored with all his heart had returned to him.* Even now his body was fiercely and vibrantly awake, after their long night of passionate lovemaking, and it was as though the force and strength of the Igazu Falls themselves were running though his veins!

But then, as if to cast a shadow over his newfound contentment, the thought came to him of how it must have been for Briana when she had first agreed to marry him and his family had all but made her feel like an unwanted usurper. *How he regretted the fact he had not spoken out against their treatment of her before!* Running his mind back over the days leading up to Briana leaving, there were two occasions that suddenly stood out like a newly lit beacon in his memory.

The first was when he had been discussing his forthcoming marriage with his mother over coffee at a hotel owned by a friend of his in Recoleta. She had made a comment to Pascual then about Briana that had made his blood boil.

'Her beauty is the kind that fades. She does not possess the extraordinary bone structure of someone like Claudia, whose beauty will only become even more exquisite as she grows older.' That was one of the things she had said, and then, *'She knows nothing of our way of life, my son…how to conduct herself in illustrious company, what clothes to wear… I would hate it if she ever embarrassed you in any way because of her ignorance.'*

If she had said those things to *him*, then had she made similar disconcerting remarks to Briana herself? he wondered painfully. If so, then it was no wonder his fiancée had felt doubtful and insecure about marrying into such a family. A family she had believed thought themselves far superior to everyone else! Given her own background, and an upper-class father who had called her his 'regrettable mistake', Pascual began to see for himself just *why* she had decided she could not go through with marrying him—even though she had professed to be in love with him.

And if she had been uncertain that she would have his support *whatever* his family thought of her, he reflected soberly, then surely he was partly to blame for her leaving? With a troubled sigh he saw his son's curly head disappear over the rise that loomed up before them, and he instantly increased his stride to catch up with him, the acute realisation bolting through his insides that he was heading towards the lake.

'Adán! Stop! Wait for me, *hijo*!'

'I want to take you to lunch.'

Briana was gazing out onto a pretty section of the vast garden filled with the most dazzling display of African violets, roses, lilies and asters from the opened patio doors in the drawing room, and Pascual's rich voice interrupted the quiet reflection she had fallen into. Her pulse leapt as he slid his arms round her waist from behind, and kissed the top of her head.

'That sounds nice…can Adán come too?'

'I want you to myself for a while, so I have asked Sofia to look after him for us. He is quite happy about the arrangement. When we return I have promised to show him the ponies.'

'I should go and get myself ready, then.'

Shyly, Briana turned so that she was facing him and, as usual, the sight of those strongly delineated handsome features, the glossy black hair and disturbing dark eyes took her breath away. Right now he was being lovely to her…considerate, kind, and—dare she say it?—*loving, even*… But how long would that last if in his heart he still couldn't forgive her for leaving?

Last night they had at least made some headway towards understanding, when Pascual had defended her against his parents. The fact that he was reflecting on his own past behaviour was a significant turning point. It meant that Briana could at last speak to him frankly and be heard. But lingering at the back of her mind was the still wounding memory of seeing him with Claudia, and the fear that she might not be enough for him even after they had married—even though he had explained that it had all been an unfortunate misunderstanding. Maybe having lunch together would be an opportune time to finally put some of her fears to bed?

'Put on something sexy for me,' he suggested now, his gaze lowering to her startled slightly opened mouth, looking as if he could eat her.

'What do you suggest? My underwear?' she

quipped, barely able to still the violent tremors that had taken hold.

'That works for me, *amante*, but I might not be able to deal with the stampede of admiring males that that would attract! Now, hurry up and get ready. We will go to Florida Street and see the street tango before we eat. I remember how much you used to love that.'

Thinking back to the many vibrant and exciting displays of street tango she had seen last time she had lived in Buenos Aires—from San Telmo to La Boca, and the more up-market end of Florida Street— Briana thought about the silky red dress she had hanging in the voluminous wardrobe upstairs. She couldn't deny the warm buzz of excitement that rippled through her at the idea of wearing it especially for Pascual…

The way the two bodies moved together was mesmerising. It was impossible to take her eyes off the woman in her short, strapless black dress, her slim, shapely legs encased in sheer black stockings and matching high-heeled shoes on her feet. Her partner was older, with a thick mane of silver hair tied back in a black band, but his lithe body moved like a much younger man's and his profile was fiercely proud. The raw sensuality of the background music, and the sight of the dancers' limbs entwining then parting—

the woman stalking away as though offended, the man striding after her and tipping her back into his arms—sent gooseflesh flying all over the surface of Briana's skin.

In the smart tiled square where a small crowd had gathered to watch the riveting display, she felt her enjoyment intimately heightened when Pascual slid his arms round her waist and drew her next to him. She could feel his heat through the thin silk of her dress, and everything in her tightened to contain the sudden flare of desire that spread like wildfire throughout her body.

'Enjoying it, *amante*?'

His voice low against her ear sent more goose-bumps flying.

'It's wonderful. They're incredible!'

'Has it sufficiently fuelled your appetite to eat now?' he teased.

'Can we stay a minute or two longer?' She turned to look at him, and he gave her one of those long, slow-burning smiles of his.

'Why not?' He shrugged, 'it pleases me to see you happy like this.'

In the restaurant afterwards, with its tall wooden-framed windows providing a perfect view of the colourful throng of passers-by—tourists and locals alike—and with the distant music of the tango still echoing in her ears, Briana excused herself to go to the ladies' room.

While she was gone Pascual found himself predisposed to smile at anyone who happened to glance his way, his contented mood of the morning easily reinstated. As he finished ordering the wine, a hand tapped him on the shoulder, and he glanced round to see his friend Diego de la Cruz and his pretty wife Marisa. After greeting them with an affectionate hug each, he invited the couple to join him.

'It is a day for bumping into old friends!' Marisa announced, settling herself in a chair, her exquisite perfume punctuating the air. 'We just saw Claudia with her new husband too.' She frowned, her slim dark brows arching. 'You *did* know she'd got married, didn't you, Pascual?'

He shrugged. 'How could I *not* know? Her wedding photos were in all the papers.'

'Once upon a time we really thought you and she would—' Her gaze narrowing briefly at her husband as she said this, Marisa quickly turned back to Pascual. 'But then you met Briana, and we knew straight away that she was the right one for you. Hearing that she was back in Palermo with you and that you have a son together was so exciting! I cannot tell you how the news lifted us.'

'I expect the news will be surprising to everyone who hears it. Initially she will be staying for a holiday, and then, when she has tied up all the loose ends in the UK, she will be moving here for good.

And you will get to meet our son soon, I promise. His name is Adán, he is absolutely amazing, and I am still feeling quite overwhelmed that he is mine.'

'Where are they now?' Diego enquired, his thoughtful gaze on his friend as the waiters bustled round behind them, serving food to the other waiting customers.

'Adán is being looked after by Sofia back at the house, and Briana has just gone to the ladies' room. She will be back at any moment.'

'There is something I must tell you before she comes back, Pascual.' Covertly, Marisa bent her dark head towards him. 'We have been friends for a long time, haven't we?'

'Where is this leading?' Immediately aware of a more serious undertone to the innocent-sounding question, Pascual felt sudden disquiet arise inside him.

'I pray you will not take offence at me saying what I am about to say, but when I heard that Briana was back with you, and that she had had your son while you were apart, I guessed why she had decided not to go through with the wedding—and I knew it was *not* because she didn't love you with all her heart!'

His chest tightening almost painfully, Pascual could hardly take his eyes off Marisa as he waited for her full explanation. 'Go on,' he said, voice low.

'Remember the party that Claudia unexpectedly turned up to with Rafa? Do you know who *really*

invited her? It was Paloma. Your mother persuaded her
to come and make mischief between you and Briana.
She was convinced Claudia was the woman you
should really be marrying, and she hoped if Briana
saw you two together she would call off the wedding
and leave the way clear for you to get back with her.'

'How do you know all this?'

'Claudia told me. She is still fond of you, Pascual,
and she only wants your happiness. She truly regrets
what happened at the party, and the idea that she
might have helped drive Briana away. Her own happiness has made her see that she did a very bad thing.
It is her hope that one day you will forgive her.'

'I can hardly believe what I am hearing.'

Feeling slightly dazed, Pascual reached for the
jug of iced water on the table and poured a glass. He
took a long draught to ease the sudden aching
dryness in his throat, then wiped the back of his hand
across his mouth. *His own mother had helped drive
away the woman he loved and consequently pre-
vented him from knowing that she had had a son by
him!* It was almost beyond belief. Now he saw that
he had been right to reflect on some of his mother's
more acerbic comments before his planned marriage.
If only he had reflected more on them at the time, he
thought again. If only he had made his feelings
towards Briana much more clear to everyone. Then
maybe his mother would have seen for herself how

much she meant to him, and would have stayed well clear from making mischief of any sort!

'Pascual?'

'It is all right, Marisa.' The semblance of a rueful smile touched his lips. 'I am not upset that you told me this. In fact…I appreciate your frankness. Too many things have been pushed under the carpet for too long, and it is time they were aired. So, thank you.'

'I thought it was you! Oh, how lovely to see you both!'

Briana had returned, the red silk dress that so lovingly complemented her gorgeous figure drawing many appreciative glances as she returned to their table, Pascual saw. And none were more appreciative than *his*.

Hugging Marisa, then a smiling Diego, she dropped back down into her seat. The elegant young woman she'd once worked for was smiling warmly, and Briana genuinely felt for the first time as though she were among friends. 'Pascual was telling me that Sabrina is quite the young lady now. I would love to see her some time, if that's possible?'

'And we would love to see your son too, Briana,' Marisa responded eagerly. 'As soon as we learned of his existence we could not wait to hear all about him. We have just been pestering Pascual for information!'

'I would talk about him all day if you want me to.' He smiled and reached for Briana's hand, gripping it as though he never wanted to let it go again.

Something in him had changed, she saw, and her heart fluttered. He was behaving more and more like the Pascual of old—the man she'd fallen head-over-heels in love with almost from the start. Now, as much as she adored seeing Diego and Marisa again, she wished they were alone so that she might enjoy his company even more, talk frankly to him about all the things that were left unsaid between them.

'A toast!'

The waiter had brought more glasses, and Pascual was busy filling them with wine.

'To good friends, and to the best of futures for all of us!'

And Briana knew in that moment that to contemplate a future without this man would be like contemplating any mother's worst fear…that of something dreadful happening to her child. It was simply unbearable and unthinkable, and if she wanted this day to end in the same optimistic spirit as this lovely moment amongst friends then she would think of it no longer…

CHAPTER ELEVEN

SOFIA and Carlo the groundsman were running towards the car as Pascual drove down the drive towards the house's main entrance.

'What's going on?' Briana glanced nervously at Pascual, but he didn't answer. He was, instead, winding down his window and leaning out, conversing in Spanish with his clearly agitated staff. Nonetheless she quickly and horrifyingly understood what the two retainers were telling him.

Adán had been playing in the garden outside the drawing room. He had lifted the latch on the gate there and disappeared into the park. Carlo had been out looking for him, but as yet had not had any luck. He had only just returned to the house to see if the boy had come back to Sofia, but he hadn't.

Briana's first thought was the lake and so—judging by the colour rapidly draining from his face—was Pascual's.

'We've got to find him!'

She grabbed at his sleeve, the bright future she'd seduced herself into believing could come true suddenly obliterated by an unseen wrecking ball that had smashed all her hopes and dreams into devastating dust.

'Trust me, *mi amor*, we will. We will go and search together. Come!'

They were out of the car and running into the park, leaving a stricken Sofia standing at the entrance and a determined-looking Carlo heading out into the expanse of forested and lush green behind them. Turning briefly, Pascual instructed the older man to expand the search into another area nearby, where Adán might have wandered.

Shouting out her son's name as she ran, the man by her side doing the same, Briana's throat was hoarse with strain and anxiety by the time they approached the rise that preceded the lake.

'I will go on ahead. Don't worry…everything will be all right. We will find him safe.' Briefly clasping her to him, clearly registering the fear and terror in her white-faced countenance, Pascual touched his lips tenderly to her brow.

'You promise?' she begged, heart pounding, not caring that she was coming unglued in front of him.

'*Con todo mi corazón!* With all my heart!'

He left her then, and the tall, lithe black trousered and white shirted figure quickly disappeared over the top of the grassy rise. Breaking into a run too, with every stride she took Briana prayed her son would be found safe and well. *If only she hadn't gone to lunch without him! If only she had got in touch with Pascual as soon as she'd learned that she was pregnant and asked him to forgive her for running away! If only...*

A million regrets and thoughts flowed unstoppably through her mind, and only when she heard her name being called with the kind of urgency that turned her limbs into cooked spaghetti did she realise she was weeping. Freezing where she stood for a moment, in the next instant she forced herself to run. At the top of the hill she glanced down, to see Pascual carrying Adán in his arms. The lake was a vast smooth mirror speared by glinting sunlight behind them. Her son was talking to his father, and she saw Pascual press the small curly head against his chest for a moment, before glancing up and waving to her. Even from a distance she saw the unrestrained joy on his handsome face, and her heart turned over with gratitude and love.

'Where did you go, Adán? I was so worried!' Out of breath, and crying at the same time, as she drew level with the smiling pair Briana grabbed her son's small hand and reverently touched his face, as if surveying its innocent beauty for the very first time.

There were smears of dirt on his flushed cheeks, but he didn't appear as though he was hurt or injured.

'I wanted to see the ponies, but then I got lost and fell down the hill, and I landed near the lake!'

'Promise me you wouldn't have gone into the water?'

'Only if I was in a boat or I had my water wings and you and Daddy were with me!'

'But *why* did you leave the garden without telling Sofia?'

'Is she cross with me, Mummy?'

'I'm sure she's not cross, sweetheart, but she's worried out of her mind. She was in charge of making sure you were safe while Daddy and I went out. Imagine what she must have felt when she looked into the garden and you weren't there!'

'I'm sorry…'

'I have already told him it was not a good idea to do what he did, and I have made him promise me that he will never do such a thing again or I will not be taking him to see the ponies. Isn't that right, Adán?'

'Yes, but you *will* take me to see the ponies when I've washed my face, won't you? You said everyone should always keep their promises!'

The child gave him such a solemn yet hopeful glance that Pascual felt his heart splinter. *He'd thought he had lost him…* Just as he had lost Fidel and then Briana when she had left him. But this potential loss—the loss of the son he had only just come to know—would have been the most heart-breaking of all. The devastation that had swept through him at the idea Adán could be dead from a fall or drowned in the lake had left him shaking, feeling as if a hurricane had tossed him high into the air and then swept his body onto jagged rocks. Now that he had discovered him safe and well, the euphoria that pumped through Pascual's bloodstream was like the headiest, most potent cocktail he had ever imbibed.

'I will take you to see the ponies, *hijo*, when your *mamà* has washed your face and hands and we have got you a drink from the kitchen.'

He turned to survey Briana, her light make-up streaked with her tears, and her face paler than he'd ever seen it. A cooling breeze had sprung up, and it plastered the thin silk of her pretty red dress against her body, teasing the silken strands of her dark hair into a gentle tangle. She was *ravishing*.

He sensed something else besides euphoria move through him, and it was equally powerful and exhilarating. *He loved this woman—heart and soul. He always had and always would—no matter what had transpired between them before.* People talked about the one they loved making them feel complete, and *that* was what he experienced being with Briana. If only he had been more open with her right from the start, had made her feel that she was safe with him, know that he would always love and protect her no matter what…then maybe she would not have run away.

After he had lost his best friend, Pascual had vowed he would be more open and honest in his relationships, would not waste time prevaricating or being inauthentic. Life was the most precious gift, and every day should be lived in acknowledgement of that. But he had *not* shared those views with the woman he loved, and consequently she had believed him to be a very different man from the one he knew himself to be. An arrogant, uncaring man who gave more credence to his status in life than nurturing the people he loved. Well, fate had given him a second chance to demonstrate the truth to her, and he would not waste another second of it in unhappiness or doubt.

'Are you all right?' he asked her.

She nodded and smiled, though her eyes were still moist. 'I'm fine. Just so relieved and grateful that he's all right!'

'Then let us go back to the house,' he said, reaching for her hand and lightly squeezing it. 'Sofia and Carlo will be anxious to know the little one is safe.'

'And *then* you can take me to see the ponies!' Adán piped up with a disarming grin.

Ruffling his curly hair, Pascual laughed and planted a kiss on his brow. 'I can see that you do not give up easily, Adán. That is a quality I very much admire. When you have a goal in life—whatever it is—you should never give up believing you can attain it.' His gaze met Briana's, and she held it for a long second before glancing away again and blushing slightly. Answering warmth curled inside him. 'So, yes, *mi hijo*…I will take you to see the ponies—just as I have promised!'

'Briana?'

The scented steam emanating from the partially opened bathroom door told him immediately where she was. Not long returned from viewing the polo ponies with his son, and having left the boy with a doting Sofia in the kitchen, eating some chocolate chip cookies that she had made especially for him, Pascual could wait no longer to see the woman he loved.

He knocked lightly on the door, and when she didn't answer, slipped off his shoes and stepped inside the room. The luxurious bath was an opulent affair, set on a marble plinth up two surrounding marble steps, and as the steam cleared Pascual saw a long pale arm draped over the side, and Briana lying with her head back and her eyes closed. *At the height of her beauty Cleopatra herself could not have looked lovelier or more desirable.* The scented water lapped gently over her luscious form amid a myriad of foamy pink bubbles, and her hair was piled on top of her head in a dark silken cloud.

Crouching down beside the bath, Pascual feasted his hungry gaze for several long, appreciative moments before dipping his fingers into the sea of bubbles, gathering a few, and touching them gently to her nose. She opened her eyes—those incredible silvery grey eyes, whose power to shake him to his very core had never diminished—and it was like gazing into a sparkling moonlit lake. 'I didn't hear you come in. I must have dozed off. Where's Adán?'

'He is with Sofia, eating cookies, and he is quite happy.'

'He'd better not eat too many or he won't eat his dinner tonight.'

'I told Sofia not to let him overdo it.'

'Is she all right now? She was so upset about Adán running off like that.'

'I reassured her that there is no blame involved, and she is fine. She literally turned her back for a minute and he was gone. In future we will all make doubly sure we watch him like a hawk. As for you dozing off, you know you should never fall asleep in the bath, *mi amor*…you might drown!'

'I always do it.' Her delectable lips parted in the most edible smile. 'And I've never drowned yet.'

'I am almost tempted to get in there with you and teach you a lesson for being so reckless with your own safety.'

'What *kind* of lesson?'

'Are you teasing me, Briana Douglas—soon to be Señora Briana Dominguez?'

In surprise, she sat bolt-upright in the bath, and Pascual watched, fascinated, as the tiny pink bubbles clung to her glistening skin and inevitably provoked the already rising heat inside him to new and unsettling temperatures.

'Are you asking me to marry you, Pascual?'

'You already know that was always my intention, *mi amor*.'

She expelled a soft sigh. 'But before you wanted to marry me because I had Adán, and you naturally wanted to assume your role as his father, not because…' The sentence drifted away unfinished.

Striving to maintain the most serious expression he could muster, Pascual frowned. 'Because what?'

'You're making this very hard for me.'

Seeing the uncertainty in her eyes, and not wanting to prolong one more second of doubt, he cupped her jaw and stroked his thumb over her damp cheekbone.

'Then I will not make it hard for you any longer, *amante*. I want to marry you because I love you with all my heart and I do not want to live without you!'

'Oh, Pascual, I love you too! I've never stopped loving you…not in all these years!'

'In that case—' his fingers were already unbuttoning his white shirt as he grinned and got to his feet

'—you leave me with no choice but to get into that bath with you.'

'Really?'

'Yes—really!'

As he settled his magnificent nude body into the bath opposite her, Briana was almost delirious with happiness and delight. *Pascual loved her! He really loved her!* She wanted to pinch herself to make sure she wasn't dreaming, but she only had to study the arrestingly handsome face before her to know that she was looking at pure, twenty-four-carat diamond reality, and the love she saw blazing at her from his gorgeous dark eyes was no fantasy.

'I was wrong to leave you like I did,' she told him now, her throat tightening with regret and not a small amount of sorrow. Seeing father and son together earlier, after Adán's frightening little escapade getting lost, had brought that home to her more than anything else. 'Can you ever forgive me, Pascual?'

He looked reflective for a moment. 'I let you down too, Briana. I should have made you know that you were more important to me than anything else in the world, and clearly I did not. If you had known that, and had been confident enough to talk to me about your fears and doubts, to confide in me about your difficult childhood, then perhaps you would have stayed, *mi amor*?'

'And if only I hadn't jumped to conclusions about

you and Claudia. If only I had confronted you with my fears instead and listened to your side of things,' she heard herself say, her heart racing slightly. 'But I was completely devastated when I thought you and she might be having an affair.'

'I have a confession to make to you about what happened that night.'

Briana stared at Pascual and hardly dared breathe. Steam from the bathwater had risen up and dampened his tanned skin with tiny little droplets of moisture. His shoulders were broad and powerful, and the eyes gazing back at her were darker than molasses. *What was he going to tell her?* That the old attraction between him and his ex had been helplessly aroused that night, and it had only been afterwards that he had regretted kissing her?

'It was as I said before…Claudia had too much to drink and more or less threw herself at me. But it was not entirely her fault.' He took a deep, steadying breath before continuing. 'My mother put her up to it. It was she who invited her to the party and got her to play up to me, because she hoped you would see her and believe that I was still attracted to her. When we saw Marisa and Diego at the restaurant today I finally learned the truth. Claudia is now happily married, and she told Marisa that she truly regrets going along with my mother's little plan. I owe you a big apology, Briana. You were right when you indicated that Paloma was less than welcoming towards you. My mother is an inveterate snob, I am afraid, and she allowed her prejudices to influence her behaviour in the worst possible way. I will be phoning her tonight and telling her in no uncertain terms what I think of what she did to you…to *us*. Please believe me when I tell you it will never happen again. If she should act with anything less than genuine warmth towards you in the future I will have no hesitation in cutting her out of our lives completely! And I know how much that would hurt her…especially now that she has seen Adán.'

'At least now we all know the truth. But I think we can extend our forgiveness towards your mother, too, Pascual, don't you? With my own mum living in the UK, Adán is going to need *both* of his grandmothers as he grows—*and* his grandfather. Can we not put the past behind us and start over again? We're young and in love and we have the most beautiful son in the world! Our future can start right here and now, if you're willing?'

'*Mi amor*, I am *more* than willing to let that be the case.'

Moving towards her, Pascual covered Briana's mouth in damp erotic kisses that made her weak with joy and desire, his hands moving over her slippery warm body with all the ardour of the most insatiable of eager lovers. And when they emerged from the bathroom, quite some time later, it was only to rekindle the flame they had stoked all over again in the bedroom...

All the dancing had made her hot. Seeking the cooler air that the early hours of the morning so blissfully provided, Briana went outside. The entrancing music of the ball faded a little the more she walked away from the house, but was still easily discernible just the same. She had left Pascual waltzing with Marisa—utterly ravishing in a glittering Venetian-style ballgown and harlequin mask studded with pearls. He was in the costume of a nineteenth-century Venetian nobleman, complete with a black velvet half-mask that made him look almost too handsome and charismatic for words!

Traditionally in Argentina, because there was such a mix of cultures, a wedding was a chance for couples to remember and pay homage to their ancestry, and as Pascual's family had originally come from Italy he had suggested the Venetian masked ball theme. *He had given her a wedding to remember*, she thought with gratitude and love, hugging herself against the suddenly cooler temperatures.

The voluminous skirts of her ivory silk ballgown wedding dress rustled a little like the wind in the trees as she walked. Wearing it, she had never felt more beautiful or feminine in her life...even though the heavily boned corset beneath the figure-hugging bodice had forced her to keep her enjoyment of the lavish banquet to a minimum, so that she could at least breathe!

Glancing behind her, she saw every window in the palatial mansion blazed with light, and the long gra-velled path that led away from the house was lit with glowing lanterns on either side. It really was like the most incredible dream. A month ago she, Adán and Pascual had travelled back to the UK, so that Briana could put her affairs in order in preparation for moving to Argentina for good, and they had brought her mother Frances back with them— for an extended holiday and to be there at her daughter's wedding.

Paloma Dominguez had been sweetness itself to Frances *and* Briana, and had even issued her daughter-in-law with a clearly genuine apology for what had gone on before. Adán had given her a new lease of life, she'd enthused, and both women had insisted on tucking him into bed tonight before coming down to the ball. Two more doting grand-mothers would be hard to find!

But the thing that had amazed and heartened Briana the most was that she had made friends here. *Genuine*, caring friends she could laugh and be herself with. Nobody looked down on her because of her background, and Pascual's family had welcomed her with open arms. She saw that she had been mistaken before in imagining she wouldn't fit in and that everyone would despise her because she'd had such a different upbringing from her wealthy husband. It made her realise that some of her fears had indeed prejudiced her into not recognising that there were good people everywhere—no matter *what* their background or history—she only had to have her eyes open to see!

She walked on to a stand of trees in the distance, silhouetted against the night sky like menacing dark sentinels. The air was full of luscious scents as well as the evocative sound of cicadas. The perfume of exotic flowers mingled with the more earthy notes of the land itself, and the legacy from the sunshine earlier in the day permeated the atmosphere with faint but subtle baked warmth.

Was that the rumble of thunder she had just heard? She came to a standstill for a moment, suddenly realising that what her ears had picked up was the distant sound of a horses' hooves not the thunderous precursor to a storm. Peering into the inky night ahead, she shivered.

A rider on a black stallion bedecked in nineteenth-century livery was heading towards her at a steady canter. Briana's heart missed a beat. She hardly knew what to make of the strange scene unfolding. But when the obscured full moon emerged from behind a bank of low-lying dark clouds above the trees, shining its ethereal light on the rider and his horse, she honestly thought she had never seen anything more spine-tingling and dramatic in her whole life!

Horse and rider pulled up beside her. *'Buenas noches, mi señora,'* a richly sensual male voice greeted her.

Wishing she had brought a shawl with her, Briana shivered again. Even though the rider wore a mask, immediately she knew it was Pascual, and she stared up at him in wide-eyed wonder behind her own ivory half-mask—a disguise that she thought made the women who wore it resemble exotic and mysterious cats.

'Pascual! I left you dancing with Marisa…how did you get away so soon?'

'This house has many secret passages and exits that you do not yet know about, *mi amor*!' There was a pleased smile in his voice. 'When I saw you leave and go outside, I also saw the perfect opportunity to spirit you away from the party and take you somewhere private, where I can be alone with my new wife!'

'Where are we going?'

Gazing down at the vision in silk and satin before him, her beautiful face partially obscured by the very sexy mask she wore, her shoulders and the tops of her breasts bared by the revealing and ravishing neckline of her gown, he felt the most delicious tension coil deep inside him—as well as pride and love. *It was true what he had said. He could not wait to get her alone.* The wedding reception had started that evening and—as tradition dictated—would continue on until breakfast. Daybreak was too far away for him to wait for the privilege of making love with his gorgeous new wife, Pascual had decided earlier, and he was not going to wait a moment longer!

'Give me your hand,' he ordered.

'You don't mean—? Pascual, I can't get up on that horse in this gown! It's impossible!'

'*Nothing* is impossible!' He laughed, and hauled her up into the saddle in front of him.

After a little patient adjusting of her voluminous gown, and sliding his arms round Briana's slender waist to reach the reins, Pascual clicked his teeth and his steed broke into another steady canter.

Directing the stallion away from the path, and crossing the wide open grassy area beside it towards the woodland that lay in darkness beyond, he murmured soft-voiced against the delicate pale lobe of Briana's ear. 'Hold on, *mi amor*. This will get us there quicker!' and he schooled his horse into a near gallop.

Yelping in fright, Briana felt her body go almost rigid in the saddle in front of him, before pressing even more deeply against Pascual's chest. 'Please don't let me fall!' she begged.

'Never!' he answered. 'I am an extremely accomplished horseman, and the last thing in the world I would do would be to let the woman I love fall or injure herself in any way when in my care.'

When they came to the spot deep within the forested area that he sought—a secluded semicircle of grass and bracken beneath the shade of some very tall trees—Pascual dismounted first, then reached up for Briana to help her down onto the soft grass. As she spilled into his arms in a warm, delectable bundle of satin and silk, the feel of her body was utterly divine to his hungry senses.

'How did you enjoy your riding adventure?' he teased, reluctantly releasing her.

'It's a wonder my legs can hold me up, they're shaking so badly!'

'Well, you will not have to stand for very much longer, my sweet…I can promise you that.'

Leading the stallion a little further away, he reached for the small bundle he had secured behind the saddle before tethering the reins to a tree branch and returning to join Briana. The bundle he had collected was a generous-sized soft wool blanket, and now he shook it out and laid it at the foot of the tree they were standing beneath.

'You think of everything!' Her expression delightfully shy, Briana walked into his arms.

*It was like walking into heaven…*Briana thought. He kissed her gently at first, then, as hunger spilled over into unstoppable need for both of them, with loving hands urged her down onto the blanket. Mindless with desire and love for the wonderful man who was now her husband, she hardly knew how they accomplished the removal of her exquisite gown, with all its tiny hooks and eyes and layers of silk, but somehow they found a way.

When Briana lay beneath Pascual wearing only a cream-coloured suspender belt and matching sheer stockings he was still more or less fully clothed, except for the silk shirt that she had feverishly pulled open so that she could touch that wonderful hard-muscled chest of his. They eagerly sought the connection and release they had both been craving all day. Suspended above her, Pascual gazed down at Briana with the most emotional glance he had ever given her, and a tiny muscle flickered at the side of his perfectly sculpted cheekbone.

'I never want to lose you again,' he vowed, his tone not quite steady.

'You won't,' Briana promised, touching his cheek and wanting to keep him right there inside her for the rest of this unbelievably magical night. 'What can I do to convince you that I'm here to stay, my love?'

'Give me another child,' he answered huskily and, turning his head, pressed his warm lips against her palm.

Not even hesitating, she let a tremulous welcoming smile lift the edges of her mouth. *'Gladly,'* she replied—and meant it with all her heart…

millsandboon.co.uk Community

Join Us!

The Community is the perfect place to meet and chat to kindred spirits who love books and reading as much as you do, but it's also the place to:

- Get the inside scoop from authors about their latest books
- Learn how to write a romance book with advice from our editors
- Help us to continue publishing the best in women's fiction
- Share your thoughts on the books we publish
- Befriend other users

Forums: Interact with each other as well as authors, editors and a whole host of other users worldwide.

Blogs: Every registered community member has their own blog to tell the world what they're up to and what's on their mind.

Book Challenge: We're aiming to read 5,000 books and have joined forces with The Reading Agency in our inaugural Book Challenge.

Profile Page: Showcase yourself and keep a record of your recent community activity.

Social Networking: We've added buttons at the end of every post to share via digg, Facebook, Google, Yahoo, technorati and de.licio.us.

www.millsandboon.co.uk

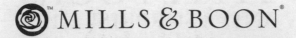

2 FREE BOOKS
AND A SURPRISE GIFT

We would like to take this opportunity to thank you for reading this Mills & Boon® book by offering you the chance to take TWO more specially selected books from the Modern™ series absolutely FREE! We're also making this offer to introduce you to the benefits of the Mills & Boon® Book Club™—

- **FREE home delivery**
- **FREE gifts and competitions**
- **FREE monthly Newsletter**
- **Exclusive Mills & Boon Book Club offers**
- **Books available before they're in the shops**

Accepting these FREE books and gift places you under no obligation to buy, you may cancel at any time, even after receiving your free books. Simply complete your details below and return the entire page to the address below. You don't even need a stamp!

YES Please send me 2 free Modern books and a surprise gift. I understand that unless you hear from me, I will receive 4 superb new books every month for just £3.19 each, postage and packing free. I am under no obligation to purchase any books and may cancel my subscription at any time. The free books and gift will be mine to keep in any case.

Ms/Mrs/Miss/Mr_____ Initials _____

Surname _____
Address _____

_____ Postcode _____

Send this whole page to: Mills & Boon Book Club, Free Book Offer, FREEPOST NAT 10298, Richmond, TW9 1BR.